Psionic Beasts
&
Women Who Must
Not Wear Purple

Michael Jay Tucker

DEDICATION

To Martha.

ALSO BY MICHAEL JAY TUCKER

And Then They Loved Him: Seward Collins and the Chimera of an American Fascism

A Promethean Heat

The Explosive-Cargo Series

A Belfort & Bastion Book.

THE UNICORN, THE MIME, THE MAN OF MIDDLE AGE

So, I'm about to give you an idea for a story.

It's a rather good one, I think. Oh, I suppose, not a great one. Not a Kafka Cockroach On The Ceiling and get a Nobel Prize and/or Tuberculosis kind of thing. But heck, how often do those come along? I mean, really?

But, it is a *good* story. In fact, that's why I'm not writing it myself. I would, you see, but it is a subtle tale, with lots of *meaning*, and wit, and humor, and chock-o-block full of symbols…I mean, real semiotic stuff like the kind that mother used to make. And, well, frankly, I'm just not up to it. I'm only a so-so writer. Good for a book or an essay or a short story or two. But the big stuff? No. I'm sorry. Not in the cards. Not even tarot cards. Not even the Fool or the Hanged Man.

Anyway, what this needs is someone with a touch of class…a surgeon rather than a butcher…a Veronica Geng, perhaps, or a Dave Berry. Or even, yes, a Dorothy Parker or E.B. White. Or, I have it, a James Thurber.

So, if you are at all like that…someone with wit and a way with the words, someone with the subtly and insight which I am so dreadfully lacking…then please step up. I'm eager for this one to get written, by someone, because it really happened to me…or part of it did.

And it goes like this.

*

Not long ago, we moved back to New Mexico because my father was getting on and needed someone to look after him. We found a delightful little house quite near his in the Northeast Heights section of Albuquerque and took up residence…the two of us, plus our dog, Oreo, a Shih Tzu of very strong opinions.

There is a park just a few steps away, just around the corner, and we walk there a lot. That's usually where I take Oreo for his morning and evening jaunts. Which does me good, too, of course. I work at home and sometimes forget to get away from my computer. He is my small but unrelenting lifestyle coach, and twice a day he insists that I take a stroll. Works out well for everyone.

A couple weeks back his coaching was particularly important. Martha, my wife, had gone back east to attend the wedding of a young woman we know. She's not (technically) family, but we think of her as a kind of adopted niece. She and our son were in the same daycare, and we've watched her grow up.

I would have liked to have gone, too. But someone had to remain home and look after Dad, so, I stayed here. The problem being that when Martha's not around, I tend to overdo, work myself day in and day out, and finish sort of exhausted. So, Oreo distracting me was uniquely valuable.

One day, shortly after I'd taken Martha to the airport and seen her on her way to Boston, I was out in the park and met a young couple walking their own dog. Call them Norton and Samantha. We ended up chatting. They had had just moved into the neighborhood. They were open and cheery, eager to meet their neighbors and make new friends.

Then, somehow, and I'm not quite certain how it came to pass, they ended up having dinner with my father and me the following night. Norton volunteered to help my father put up a ceiling lamp in his house, and I brought pizza. Then, a few days later, partly because I felt I owed them for being so kind, Dad and I had them over to my house for barbeque.

Afterwards, we promised one another in person and via electronic means that we would all get together as soon as my wife got back from Boston.

*

Okay, now let's skip ahead a few days. Martha returned from our friend's wedding. She was a little exhausted. It had been a whirlwind tour, seeing old friends, racing from Rhode Island to New Hampshire. Meanwhile, I'd come down with a flu of some sort, and neither of us was in any position to socialize.

Our young couple, meanwhile, had likewise gotten busy. They'd started their new jobs…each was working in the city…and then there were all sorts of chores to attend to. Their furniture, for instance, had not come on the promised date, and they spent a major part of their last free weekend either buying temporary furnishings (an airbed, for instance) or fighting with the moving company that had been remiss. Plus, of course, they were making new friends among their co-workers, being invited here and there, and otherwise building new relationships and discovering the city and its attractions.

So it was that our good intentions about getting together just didn't work out. We tried three or four times to set up a meeting for dessert and coffee, but *things* got in the way. Such is the story of all our lives in the postindustrial age.

And speaking of stories, we finally come to the one I hope you will tell…

*

One afternoon, after the fourth or fifth failed attempt to arrange a meeting with the young couple, I realized that they had never met or seen Martha. Oh, I'd told them about her…said that she was on the East coast, that she was a retired professor at Tufts, that she had been a high school teacher and had gone on to get her Ph.D.

But they had not *seen* her.

Which struck me as an interesting plot point. It would make for an amusing short story, a piece of fiction, and the one I hope you tell…

It begins like this: A young couple moves into a new neighborhood. They meet a Middle Aged Man walking in the park. He tells them that his wife is away. They become friendly. They come to dinner a couple of times. They also meet his aged but fascinating father (a former physicist, a real estate maven, a charming gentleman…"your father is so *cute*" Samantha tells the Middle Aged Man.)

All seems to be well.

Then, the wife supposedly comes home. The Middle Aged Man assures the Young Couple that she (the wife) is eager to meet them, and that they all must get together soon.

But somehow…somehow…it just doesn't happen. Time and time again, the planned meetings don't come to pass. There are always plausible excuses—she has a meeting at her church, she is not feeling well, his father has some unexpected complication that needs to be attended.

Gradually, the young couple becomes uneasy.

*

Actually, there is nothing sinister underway. The excuses are legitimate. The wife came home from the east and really was so tired that it took her two or three days to recover. She simply did not have the energy to be social in that period. Besides, well, she is shy and while she is capable of fearlessly commanding a meeting or a classroom, encounters with strangers in a social setting are difficult for her.

Then, too, there is the fact that she is an Easterner. She grew up in Boston and Providence. And while she is not in any way standoffish, she does have a slightly different conception of friendship and how friends are made than does her husband. Friends, in her view, are made slowly. They begin as *acquaintances*. They are first met in certain specified locations—at work, at church, in other similar settings. Then, gradually, there is the drawing together of the threads of trust and amity. Only then, and maybe a year or two after the initial contact, does one take the dangerous plunge into social intimacy. Only when one is absolutely certain that there is no chance of rejection do invites go out...for coffee, for dessert, for a chat. It is as formal and set as the intricate ballet by which the haut Frenchwoman goes from *vous* to *tu*.

The idea that one might just meet someone on the street...and decide they're "friends" ...well, seems a bit rushed, somehow. A dreadful hurry. Unsettling.

*

Besides, she's busy. Her husband still works, but he does so from home. He can leave his computer any time. The documents he edits and the clients he meets via email will always be there on his return.

Not her. She's retired, in theory, but as is the case with many retirees she actually works harder now than she ever did before. She's volunteered for many different organizations, ranging from Big Sisters to her newfound (and very liberal) church. Thus she is always rushing off to this meeting or that gathering. She has to get the Emergency Response Plan (ERP) competed so it may be presented to the congregation next month. Bill, the minister, asks could she possibly take a position on the committee for worship. And then the church administrator became ill and someone had to take his place. At least temporarily.

*

All of this is very different from the situation of her husband. As we already noted, he works at home and sees very few people other than his wife, his father, and the occasional neighbor. And while he isn't exactly lonely (he is not a particularly social person), he does now and then find himself having extended conversations with his desk lamp. And he has discovered that, like a lot of freelancers, his most frequent human contact is often the UPS guy who delivers rewrites.

Moreover, he is something of a nerd (or "nurd," depending on your choice of spelling of that useful word) and confesses openly that he therefore has somewhat limited social skills. And what few he has have begun to flitter away in the solitary confinement that is attendant upon his profession. He is clumsy in his approaches to other people. Thus it is that sometimes, *sometimes*, not always but frequently, his friendly overtures come across as …as…. well…. just a little strange. People find themselves, just perhaps, just maybe, thinking that the Middle Aged Man is, ah, an odd little twit.

In fact, downright bizarre…

*

At first, the young couple accepts the many excuses that the Middle Aged Man provides for their inability to link up. But gradually, they find themselves growing just a bit confused. There is just something a little creepy about the way he (the Middle Aged Man) is so very, very eager to "get together for coffee and desert. And you can meet my wife…" and yet, time and time again, at the very last minute, "Oh, sorry, something's come up." Or, "she's very tired and not feeling well." And "could we reschedule? She needs to do a committee thing for her church."

They began to wonder just what the heck is going on.

Meanwhile, they have begun to meet new people, make new friends…friends of their own ages and background. One day, they give a party for some of these individuals—people from their workplaces and their new neighborhood. It is all very friendly and pleasant, and by the time they've gotten to the third cup of coffee and the cheesecake, everyone's begun to share stories. And so it is, finally, that the couple elects to reveal their concerns about the Middle Aged Man and his mysteriously invisible wife. Samantha tells the tale while Norton provides the occasional clarifying detail. "It's just so, you know, *strange*…" she concludes.

It so happens that among her listeners is a gentleman who has a vivid imagination. In another life, had circumstances been slightly different, he would have been an author of mystery novels. Or tales of blood chilling horror. As it is, he is a realtor with a big agency downtown.

He hears the story. His fecund intellect rushes to complete the plot. "I'll bet…I'll bet…she doesn't even *exist*."

"What?" says the couple in unison, not believing what they're hearing.

"I bet she isn't real. You know, like those crazy cat lady women who pretend they have children. But they don't. You know, and like, you hear the baby crying in the crib, and they're always rushing off to 'feed the baby,' but actually it is just a doll with a recording on a timer."

"Ewee ick," they say. "And you think…?"

"He made her up. The wife. She's just in his imagination. You know, like *delusional*."

"But we met his father," they object. "He was real."

"Yes, but he's like, what? A hundred years old or somethin'? Maybe he's like, you know, gaga, and he doesn't realize that his daughter-in-law doesn't exist. Or, maybe…maybe…he's in on it. He knows his son is stark raving mad and he humors him."

For a moment, the young couple is tempted to believe this story. Fortunately, their common sense is stronger than the appeal of this morbid fantasy. Occam's Razor suggests that the simplest answer is the most likely. And to assume that the Middle Aged Man is sufficiently lunatic to create a completely imaginary family requires a good deal of unnecessary complexity in one's interpretation.

Thus, they reject the story. (Yet…yet…maybe they will exercise a little more caution when they see the Middle Aged Man walking his dog in the park. Maybe they will be not quite so eager to call across the grass and invite him to join them on their stroll with their own dog.)

But, even if the young couple does not believe the tale of the Middle Age Man with the imaginary wife ("…kind of *Lars And The Real Girl*, you know? The movie?") the story now assumes a life of its own. The real estate agent-qua-novelist repeats his suggestion at other gatherings. A friend of a friend conveys it to an acquaintance who reports it to a second cousin who relays it to all her BFFs and Facebook connections. Soon, it's all over the apartment complex at the intersection of Academy and Rolling Hills. Then, it leaps to the gated community (quarter acre estates) next to the golf course. And, after that, it swings back West and across to the Home Owners' Association around the elementary school. There are whispers in the PTA meetings.

And the narrative grows as it goes.

*

Now, we'll throw in an additional complication. In the medium-sized western city in which this story takes place, there has recently been a series of unexplained murders.

As the writer, you have a choice at this point. If you wish this tale to be grim and serious…that is, if you wish it to be "realistic"… then we can make these murders genuinely frightening. At various times and various places in the city, solitary young men have been waylaid and shot dead in the night. The police believe this to be gang related violence, or even a war between the various organized crime groups that control methamphetamine production and distribution in the area. (*Breaking Bad*, etc.) And this is, in fact, the actual explanation. In a few months, the conflict will die down, bodies will not be so numerous, and the tense peace that is the norm for urban areas in the postindustrial age will return.

But, for a variety of reasons, another (incorrect) theory has been advanced in some conservative quarters. The city is in the midst of a debate over gay marriage. Certain individuals with axes to grind have worked diligently to portray homosexuals as being dangerous and unpredictable. Therefore, in some quarters, you hear that the deaths are the work of a perverted serial killer who targets young men in the night.

And what would be the characteristics of said serial killer? The self-described experts answer: a man, someone who lives utterly alone, someone who seems just a little odd, a bit creepy, nursing an older relative, perhaps pretending to be married to conceal his actual perversion…

These theories are reprinted in a certain local paper.

*

Too grim? Okay. You're the writer. I'm just providing the outline. So, let's make it something other than death in the night. Let's say that in our Western city, there is a large park-qua-public space downtown. It was designed to be a place where people might go to escape the tensions of the day and the pressures of the workweek.

Alas, as is in the case in many such planned spaces, the park has become infested with undesirables. Specifically, *mimes*. A great predatory host of them has come east from California and taken up residence in the park. They put out hats and guitar cases for "donations" and then enclose themselves in invisible boxes, struggle against invisible winds, pull on invisible ropes, and otherwise harass passersby who only want to get out of the office for a minute, damn it, and for Crying Out Loud, is there *any* place where you can have a little peace these days? (Answer: no.)

Also, sometimes, the mimes follow the aforesaid passersby, imitating their motions, and mocking them…

So bad has it gotten that finally one exasperated visitor, an otherwise perfectly meek as milk toast accountant for the city public schools, is accosted and mimed on the way back from a trip to the grocery store. In a moment of blinding fury, the accountant whips out a large loaf of Italian bread and whacks the bejeesis outta the mime. (And, yes, here I'm stealing from Berkeley Breathed and the comic strip *Bloom Country*. You'll recall that in 1986 or 1985, Breathed had his Opus the Penguin similarly beat the snot out of a mime, albeit with a olive loaf. As I always say, if you're going to steal, steal from the very best.)

Our accountant, horrified at what he/she done, then dropped his/her loaf and fled in a flurry of breadcrumbs. EMTs arrived and carted the mime away to the Shriners' Hospital For Whacked Street Performers. TV stations and newspapers all went wild. Alas, the whacked mime was unable to make a statement for the police or the media and upon questioning had to restrict himself to an invisible tear.

The city is in terror. Who is the mime whacker? Will he whack again? And if so, which mime?

A police sketch artist produces an image of the alleged attacker. It shows a small, Middle Aged Man with sandy hair going gray.

The sketch is shown on TV. It is posted to the web and printed out by hundreds of citizens with color printers. Some of these printers are owned by members of the neighborhood association.

*

At this point, our young couple must (sad to say) gracefully exit our tale. There are two reasons for this. First, they have served their purpose. They were necessary to begin the chain of events that will lead finally to our ironic conclusion, but from hence forward the plot can creak and clank along perfectly well without them. This, of course, is in spite of what they tell you in creative writing classes and books about story structure where the absolutely inflexible doctrine is "Thou Shalt Not Abandon A Character!" If you begin with a one-eyed, left-handed, mime-whacking amateur taxidermist with bad breath, then, by God! you shall end with him.

But the reality is that in fiction, as in life, more often than not our connections, friends, enemies, even relations tend to drift in and out and in and out again of our lives. One moment they loom large in our existence...the next, they are not even a memory.

Besides, and here is the second reason, as I say, I really know the young couple upon whom these two imaginary people are based. I do not wish to offend by making them the villains of the piece. So I will now quietly draw the curtain, lower the veil, hush their voices...

And lo! They are gone from our history.

*

We pick up the action a few days later. The driver of the plot now is an informal or semi-formal Committee of Public Safety which has been formed in the area around the home of our Middle Aged Man. It has given itself the title of Greater Northeast Heights Association for the Protection of Our Children and the Prevention of the Whacking of Innocent Mimes ...or GNHAPOCPWIM for short.

GNHAPOCPWIM meets regularly in the garage of a certain local semi-celebrity, a man who is *supposed* to be the veteran of a particular nasty foreign war. He can always be counted upon to provide tales of combat and glory, and to display his various medals. In fact, he spent the war typing triplicate copies in a depot in Prosaic, East Jersey, and the medals he purchased at pawnshop down on Central where they'd been left by a genuine albeit now homeless hero who discovered (alas) that a Grateful Nation was delighted to Thank Him For His Service…and then let him rot on the street when it found out he was jobless and suffered from a little case of PTSD.

Anyway, the Old Soldier tells the committee members at an emergency session one evening, "We know of course he's a pervert freaky crypto-commie, but is he a Mime-Whacker? And if so, what do we do about him?"

At this point the vice president of the committee, a professor of Applied Social Paranoia at the University of Advanced Postmodernist Gibberish, speaks up condescendingly, making it sound (somehow) as if she is correcting him even though she isn't. She talks to everyone that way. "Well, naturally," she says, "it is important to be absolutely certain about guilt before presuming innocence. But…" She pauses thoughtfully, then resumes, "But, it really doesn't matter because the mere possession of a middle class background and/or Y-chromosome is *eo ipso* to be guilty of a myriad of macro-, medio-, and micro-aggressions. Ergo, we may assume that even should he be (in bourgeois terms) 'innocent'… we may act as if we were guilty as sin in any case."

There is a momentary silence while the other committee members digest this fascinating communication. Then, as a man, they turn to the unofficial secretary of the organization, Sam the Shrink, the psychotherapist who has an office in the big building on Montgomery. He pauses to dramatically to light his pipe. (Actually, he hates tobacco. But he has found the Meerschaum an invaluable affectation, implying a profundity that he in no way actually possesses.) "Well…" he says, finally, and all eyes are on him. "Well…"

He pauses. He waits. He closes his eyes. He opens them again. He smiles. Smoke dribbles out his nostrils.

"Well," he repeats. Then he adds, "I think we may be certain that we are dealing with an extremely neurotic, not to say *disturbed* individual, doubtlessly manifesting such symptoms of mental ill-health as antisocial behavior, adjustment disorders, body dysmorphia, cognitive malfunction, Diogenes syndrome, gender identity problems, Ganser syndrome, Hallucinogen persisting perception disorder (HPPD), Persecutory delusions, Social anxiety, Schizoaffective disorder, Transvestophilia, Triskaidekaphobia, Zoophilia, and, of course, Mime-Whacking."

There is another silence. Finally the Old Soldier speaks, "What the fuck does that mean?"

Sam the Shrink extracts his pipe from his clinched teeth. He regards it. He realizes it's gone out. He strikes another match. Sucks to get the sulfur taste. Then speaks, "It means, ladies and gentlemen, that we have a Booby in our midst. And we ought to take him to the Booby Hatch."

*

You are, of course, a sophisticated individual. You have read much. You recognize in the paragraph above this one the respectful borrowing (a.k.a., blatant plagiarism) from James Thurber's classic short story, "The Unicorn in the Garden."

I'm so glad we could share this moment of advanced literary appreciation.

*

Now, before we can proceed we must take a moment to provide yet another bit of background. To wit, the Middle Aged Man's wife has a ...ah...*strained* relationship with the telephone. It is not her favorite technological innovation.

She...for sake of convenience, let's call her Martha...was a bit of a hippie in her younger days, and early on she conceived a distaste for the jangling little fiend of cords and connections which intruded into every setting and refused to take no for an answer. She hated the fact that her parents (and so many of their generation) were virtual slaves of the device, dashing across the room or rushing up stairs at its demanding and demeaning summons to talk to someone who, almost certainly, you really didn't want to talk to in the first place.

Why didn't people understand, she asked, that all you had to do was refuse to answer? That was all. And you were free.

As time went on, and cell-phones appeared, her distaste grew more intense. Now people lugged phones about with them. They called and answered calls in *every* situation and *every* location. Parks, gardens, restaurants, art galleries...all were subject to Mr. Bell's monster. It was maddening, vulgar, and ridiculous.

She herself did purchase a cell phone, finally, at the insistence of her husband, who said it was a useful thing to have, and you never could tell when you might get stranded and need to call AAA or something. She agreed with that. At least the conscious part of her did so. However, the other part, the truer self, the unconscious part that dreamed of communes and Walden Pond and all the Transcendentalists in their poetic majesty...well, that other part of her fought back tooth and nail. Covertly, perhaps, but fiercely. Thus it was that she was constantly "forgetting" to take the phone when she left the house. Or, if she did, well, by golly, somehow she'd neglected to charge it and the battery was as deceased as the proverbial dodo on roller skates. Or, if it was charged, then (gosh, how did that happen?) she oh-so-accidentally pushed the "wrong" button and so disconnected the caller and/or erased the message forever and ever. And *ever*. And naturally Martha was far too genteel to whisper something like "fuck you, you electronic asshole," while she "accidentally" did these things, but there are those who claim to have seen a certain gleam in her eye at the time.

*

Okay, now it is necessary to relate all this background because a short time later we come to the night before the day that is the climax of our little tale. Specifically, it is a Tuesday. Martha knows that she has an important meeting at her church on Wednesday. They are finalizing a significant report to the congregation on how the Church should respond in the event an emergency. Like a terrorist attack or a madman with a gun. Martha's church is a left-wing church, and therefore all too likely a target of such things.

Atypically on this night before, she recalls that her phone is in need of charging. She therefore puts it on the charger where she's left it on the counter in the kitchen next to the toaster. Where the damn thing might "accidentally" someday get incinerated. But, that hasn't happen yet. (Not for want of trying.)

The next morning, the phone is nicely charged. Martha, however, is in a terrible, terrible hurry because she gets up a little late and dashes out the door…

Leaving the phone behind.

*

Her husband, the Middle Aged Man, walks the dog and then turns to his labors. He is editing a manuscript that is so bad that it could curdle milk at thirty yards. (Roughly 30 meters for those outside the US of A and related territories.) The tale had something to do with elves, aliens, female CEOs of global corporations, and an extremely muscular guy who, for no particularly good reason wears a cowboy hat, leather chaps, and no shirt a lot.

Alas, the Middle Aged Man is being paid to edit this remarkable piece of literature and so cannot do the logical and reasonable thing and drag the electronic file to his Mac's trashcan and hit DELETE while taking the printout and using it as inexpensive albeit somewhat uncomfortable alternative to Mr. Whipple's favorite paper product. (Look him up, ye of youthful years. He's on Wikipedia.)

So, the Middle Age Man must, instead, crank his way through the tragic prose without chance of relief except for occasional breaks to scream obscenities at the top of his lungs and/or pound his head repeatedly on the wall. Which is unfortunate since the wall is rather soft one, constructed of frame and sheet rock, and is thus in serious danger.

During one of the more vociferous screaming sessions, the doorbell rings. The Middle Aged Man is surprised (no one ever visits during the day) but not displeased. It's a chance, after all, to get away from the female CEO and her half naked cowboy who are even now banging away like a couple of frenzied weasels on d-meth in some public place, probably in Paris, with an interested (and growing) circle of spectators who now and then applaud the energy and technique of the couple at their most elastic.

The Middle Aged Man opens the door and finds himself facing a committee of total strangers who include The Old Soldier, The Full Professor of Applied Social Paranoia, Sam The Shrink, assorted other members of the GNHAPOCPWIM, several policemen, a nice selection of highly muscular individuals wearing stereotypical white jackets and carrying butterfly nets, and, of course, a much bandaged Mime with a sour expression on his face.

Startled and confused, the Middle Aged Man asks, "May I help you?"

Sam the Shrink acts as a spokesman for the group. "We need to speak to your wife," he says.

Still confused, the Middle Aged Man replies, "I'm sorry, but she's not here right now."

"Ah ha," says Sam the Shrink. "That's very significant. And where is this alleged wife of yours."

"She's at a meeting. We can phone her if you like."

"Ah ha," says Sam again. "What's her number?" He extracts his cell phone from an inner pocket.

The Middle Age Man is, alas, forgetful and he has to take out his own cell phone and check the number on his contact list. Sam the Shrink, the Old Soldier, The Professor, and all the GNHAPOCPWIM members nod to one another. This, too, is *significant.*

Finally, though, the number is read out. Sam dials. Everyone jumps as the sound of a phone ringing in the kitchen can be clearly heard. Two policemen check and bring back the offending phone in a plastic evidence bag.

"So you see," Sam says to the Old Soldier, The Professor, the GNHAPOCPWIM members, the police, and muscular men in white, and the Whacked Mime, "the evidence is overwhelming. There is no Wife. Only a carefully constructed figment of the diseased imagination of this unfortunate if seriously and dangerously disturbed individual."

"Pardon me?" says the Middle Aged Man.

"I mean," says Sam, "you are a Booby. And we are going to take you to the Booby Hatch." Then, at the signal from of the policemen, the individuals in white jump on the Middle Aged Man and, in a great flurry of butterfly nets and straight jackets, drag him kicking and screaming out the door.

After that, Sam the Shrink, Old Soldier, The Professor, the GNHAPOCPWIM members, the police, and the Whacked Mime, congratulate one another on a job-well-done and go away. It is the Whacked Mime who remembers to lock the door.

*

And after that? Ah, we have an excellent opportunity for a bit more comedy. Though, of course, we once again must exercise caution…indeed, a great deal of it. Because, it will come at the expense of Martha, and I am (after all) married to the woman, and it is an extremely good idea not to piss off someone who lives in the same house as one's self, and who may be, at some point in the near future, awake when one is asleep. (This is a tip. Write it down.)

So, we will begin with a disclaimer. What follows is not Martha. Rather, it is *fictional* Martha, a creature completely, utterly, and totally unrelated to the original. And any resemblance is entirely co-incidental. And unintentional. Got that? Good. Let's go.

*

The fictional Martha comes home. She is not surprised to find herself alone. Her husband is often out in the late afternoons…taking care of his father, going to coffee shops to work in the relative peace of the public space, getting a bit of exercise (in summer months, he frequently goes up for a jog to the Bear Canyon Arroyo, whose John B. Robert dam has been made famous by *Breaking Bad*).

So, weary after the long day at church and her various activities, she fixes a cold drink, removes her shoes and sinks gratefully into her recliner…there to read the paper or work on a crossword puzzle. She is joined shortly by the dog who curls up and sleeps soundly next to her thigh.

And just as she has gotten to the section on Broadway Openings (they subscribe to the *Times*), or begun her battle with 42 Down ("A sixteen letter word meaning 'pathetic fallacy.'") the phone rings. Not her cell phone. But the landline. The one on the wall in the kitchen. *Ring. Ring. Ring.*

It is a jarring, unwelcome noise. *Damn.* She decides to ignore it. After all, she *just* got *comfortable*. And, she is *tired.* And it's been a long day. *Ring. Ring. Ring.*

And her legs hurt, and her feet hurt, and she's got the beginnings of a headache…and the arthritis in her thumb is acting up. And, anyway, it is almost surely just a sales call. And even if it isn't, they'll leave a message. *Ring. Ring. Ring.*

She assumes the caller will give up after a moment. But the phone continues its summons. *Ring. Ring. Ring.* It is annoying. It is unpleasant. She grits her teeth. Will they never get the hint? *Ring. Ring. Ring.* Apparently not. *Ring. Ring. Ring.* The caller refuses to do the graceful thing and hang up. *Ring. Ring. Ring.*

Who on earth could it be at this time of night? *Ring. Ring. Ring.* Really, there ought to be a *law* against telemarketers. *Ring. Ring. Ring.* It's institutionalized rudeness, that's what it is. *Ring. Ring. Ring.* The gross materialism of American Society...enough to make you weep. *Ring. Ring. Ring.* The endless selling...the lack of serenity...the intrusion... *Ring. Ring. Ring.*

Finally, her patience exhausted, she heaves herself up out of the chair...disturbing the dog and dropping the paper while her favorite crossword pen rolls under the coffee table. *Ring. Ring. Ring.* She takes the time to reclaim the pen and the paper. Then— *Ring. Ring. Ring*—she begins the long and arduous journey to the kitchen where the phone is on the wall. *Ring. Ring. Ring.*

She comes finally to the phone's base station. *Ring. Ring. Ring.* She glances at the caller ID. There is no name, just a number. *Ring. Ring. Ring.* It is a 505 area code, meaning that it is local number, but she's never seen it before. *Ring. Ring. Ring.* Could it be one of her church contacts? No. Probably not. *Ring. Ring. Ring.*

Could it be one of her Massachusetts friends? No, they would have 781 or 617 numbers. *Ring. Ring. Ring.* Who could it be? Who could it be? She racks her memory. *Ring. Ring. Ring.* Could it be her doctor? No. *Ring. Ring. Ring.* Her dentist? No. *Ring. Ring. Ring.* One of the neighbors? No. *Ring. Ring. Ring.*

Her hand hesitates over the receiver. *Ring. Ring. Ring.*

Oh, hell, she says, all right. She lifts the handset from its cradle. "Hello," she says.

"Click," she hears in return. Then silence.

Phooey, she thinks. And then, taking a moment to refresh her iced coffee, she returns to the recliner and her puzzle.

*

It had been, of course, her husband on the phone, desperately dialing her up from the Booby Hatch. He had talked one of the Men in White Coats into giving him one last chance to prove the existence of his wife. But, when there was no answer, the Man in question said, "Right, that's it

14

for you then," and the husband is dragged (once again, kicking and screaming) off to a padded cell. (Cue the laugh track.)

And that's where we *should* end this story, but, unfortunately, it just doesn't work that way. The story simply cannot end in such a fashion. For one thing, there aren't that many publicly supported Booby Hatches around any more. During the Reagan years, we got tired of paying for mental hospitals. So, in the name of civil liberty and cost reduction, we closed them all down and tossed the residents into the street. Ergo, there are few padded cells for our hero, the Middle Aged Man, to be thrown into.

Also, it is illogical. Eventually, no matter how tired she was, the wife would realize her husband wasn't coming home. There would follow most un-comedic scenes of panic. Eventually, after a few hours of desperate searching, she learns the fate of her spouse from a helpful neighbor who had witnessed the police, the Men In White, the committee members, Sam the Shrink, the Professor, the Old Soldier …and, oh, yes, the Middle Aged Man in a straitjacket.

A few phone calls later and she's down at the station house or the mental hospital getting her husband out of durance vile. And, in the process, providing some choice words to various authority figures (never her favorite type of human) about just exactly where they can insert their assorted legal procedures, moral interventions, butterfly nets, court orders, and nightsticks.

From there, of course, we may proceed rapidly to the conclusion of our story…or, rather, "your" story, because you're the one who will be writing it. Though, perhaps, you will forgive me if I throw in a couple more suggestions.

For example, there is another good comic scene to be had when the Greater Northeast Heights Association for the Protection of Our Children and the Prevention of the Whacking of Innocent Mimes (GNHAPOCPWIM) has its next meeting. The whole gang is there, and particularly the Old Soldier, the Snotty Professor, and Sam The Shrink. They are applauding themselves regarding their masterful handling of the Mime Whacking Pervert who'd been living in their midst.

Suddenly, there is a hush. Collectively, they realize that standing in the open doorway of the garage is a stranger.

They look. It is a sinister figure. A man who looks like something out of…oh, The *Godfather*. Or, better yet, *Breaking Bad*—maybe the "Cousins." In fact, we'll make it two people. Two baldheaded guys in shiny suits and wearing cowboy boots that come with little skulls on the toes. (Damn! But Vince Gilligan is good that sort of thing.)

And, anyway, the two guys have bulges in ominous places. And, believe me, it's not cause they're glad to see you. In the chill silence, they reach inside their coats. Everyone cringes. But it isn't pistols that are produced. It is a Legal Notice. The committee members discover they are being sued for ten million bucks.

The two bald-headed guys go away. The committee members stare in shock. After a very long time, someone says something. Maybe it is Sam The Shrink. What he says is, "Oops." It is as profound a statement as he will ever make.

The case will be settled out of court. Martha, the Middle Aged Man, and his Father will move out of town...in fact, to a comfortable little island that has remarkably lax regulations about the taxation of foreign residents.

And that's where the story ends.

*

It is, of course, ridiculous.

Oh, I don't mean the story itself. Admittedly, the tale is full of absurdities. The Mime Whacker is ridiculous. The name of the committee of public safety is silly. But, no, the *real* issue...the genuine failing... is the happy ending. We know that would never occur. Not in real life. In real life, the Middle Aged Man, no matter how falsely accused, how unjustly slandered, would be destroyed. His face would appear in endless cable news programs, his name invoked in countless editorials...

And even if he were proven innocent, well, please, let us be honest. What happens to those who become the foci of our witch-hunts and public burnings? Our Central Park Fives, our Duke Lacrosse Teams, our Fells Acres Day Care Providers...?

Answer: they are allowed to hang in the wind. No one apologizes. No one admits an error. A little money may, on occasion, be awarded for pain and suffering. But the damage is done. In the public mind, forever and ever, guilt has been established and there is no escaping.

Innocence of the crime, like ignorance of the law, is no excuse.

*

But, naturally, we cannot...you and I, we joint authors of this piece...allow such thoughts to intrude into our otherwise merry little tale. No. We must be cheery and bright. We must have likeable characters and a happy ending, with plenty of room for product placement in the middle. Otherwise, there's no chance of it getting picked up by Hollywood. No possibility of a sitcom.

Ah well. Such is life.

*

And so we come to the end. I have no more to offer. This is the story I wish you to tell.

Please do so soon. I am looking forward to reading it. I would love to see how a genuine artist would handle the material. Will you do it *a la* slapstick? Will you be serious? Will it be funny or grim? Might there be, perhaps, many versions? Could it be that there are multiple artists out there, multiple writers, or even poets and filmmakers and cartoonists, who will each turn to this material and make of it something good?

Well…only time will tell.

*

I will, however, leave you with one final anecdote. You might be able to use it…and, again, this really happened…though, for reasons of drama, I shall relate the tale as though it happened to someone else.

You see, Norton and Samantha finally *did* meet Martha…though (as of the moment I write this), we've still yet to get together for dessert and coffee. Everyone's calendar is so busy.

But, one evening, Samantha was riding her bike home from work. I happened to be (once again) walking the dog…this time in the gathering dark. Oreo and I met her and on the street and we took her to meet Martha. It was all very charming and pleasant, and I think the two women liked each other.

Then, a week or so later, Samantha sent Norton over with a side-dish for our Thanksgiving Dinner…a yam thing, with nuts on the top. It was quite good and we enjoyed it greatly.

But, when Norton brought the yams, that was the occasion of the last part of the tale.

It happened as follows: The doorbell rings. Martha answers it as her husband emerges from his home office. It is Norton. He hands off the yam dish. There are introductions and witty remarks.

Michael, the Middle Aged Man, makes a joke. "See," he says, "she really exists." Meaning Martha. "And you thought I was just delusional."

Norton laughs and, falling into the spirit of the thing, following the lead of the Middle Aged Man, also jokes. "I thought it was going to be like Psycho and I'd turn the chair around and…"

Suddenly, the Younger Man stops. He is horrified because he realizes his joke might be taken as an insult…an implication that Martha might be, well, you know, less than living. Might appear the skull.

Martha is, in fact, not in the least offended. She may not even notice the remark. But the Younger Man is aghast as his own faux pas…the misstep that he may or may not have taken, but which reduces him now to the sort of anguished paralysis one feels in such situations. That haunting, horrible sense of My God, My God, why did I say *that*?

The Middle Aged Husband...who has been in exactly the same situation so many times, has quivered so often with a similar anguish, and who realizes that he is at least partially responsible for the situation because he began the joke, ...leaps to the rescue. He changes the subject. Mentions something else. Norton, with relief, turns to the new topic...delighted that an innocent remark or act, by which nothing offensive was meant, will not be used as a weapon against him.

Everyone smiles and nods and agrees that just as soon as they have a chance, they will do dessert. And coffee. Some evening. Very soon.

And then Norton goes home again.

*

As I say, it is a minor addition to the tale. Perhaps not worth telling. But, I could be wrong in that. You are, I know, of the clever sort, creative, possessed of a vast capacity for fictive invention... maybe you will be able to work it into your narrative. Maybe you'll be able to make it, somehow, significant.

Why, who can say?

Throw in a garden or a lily, and you might even have a metaphor. For something. Or other. Though for precisely what...

Well, I'll leave that you.

After all, you're the author.

I'm just here for the unicorns.

BUGS. HYGIENE

When you were a very young man and a very new father, you had—you were told —a personal hygiene problem. Or, more precisely, the story had to do with insects.

To explain: you worked for a computer trade magazine downtown at a big publishing company. You had just moved to Boston some months before, fleeing a job at another trade rag, this one in New Hampshire, that had collapsed into bankruptcy following the management's failure to adapt to the changing nature of the computer industry. (They'd remained dedicated to CP/M boxes even as IBM clones became the dominant choice of the industry. This was, you see, the very early '80s.)

And you'd gotten the new job and moved . . . while your wife was in the final two months of pregnancy. You'd been in a desperate rush to find a place to live in a seller's market and so, somehow, the two of you found yourselves in a hot, run-down, dreadful little upper story apartment in a depressed town up the coast.

You had to take two buses and a train to get to work, and the commute actually took a bit out of your hide . . . but you did not complain because you knew it was cream and cake compared to what your wife went through then, when your son was born by Caesarian section. And then, your newborn had colic (he slept for less than three hours at a time at any one stretch, which meant that you and she did the same), and your mother-in-law came to "help." Which was a disaster, because while she meant well, the woman was old and in profound ill-health (she threw her back out the day she arrived), and she was not over-fond of either you, or of the baby, who came between her and her daughter, the focus of her entire emotional and social life these many years, since the death of her husband.

Indeed, the very worst moment of your life (at least so far) came when you returned home from your hour and a half bus commute to find your wife—exhausted, white skinned with fatigue—standing at the stove, crying baby under one arm, cooking dinner for her mother, who sat at the kitchen table smoking and reading a mystery novel. (You had made your wife sit down and you finished the meal preparations. Though you never, ever forgave yourself for letting the situation occur in the first place.)

But ...

*

But the bugs. And how they came to say you stank.

First, it should be admitted that they might have a point. Not that you were really odiferous. No. But, you were a bit disheveled at this time, new father, new parent. Exhausted. Scented with diaper powder and bus fumes. Sometimes you forgot to comb your hair.

But you were clean. You bathed.

*

Now, more background.

The publishing company owned its own building downtown. The place was a great, box-like structure of stone that had once, or so the story went, been a bicycle factory. It was quite crowded—the company had out-grown it long ago, every floor boasted one or two magazines and a newsletter at least.

There was also a basement which was used for what is colorfully referred to as "Dead Storage," that is, things which should be thrown away, but aren't . . . back issues of defunct titles, payroll records of long departed (in some cases, deceased) employees, tax forms from unremembered administrations.

It, too, was crowded, though not with human inhabitants. A large population of rats lived there. And enormous roaches. Sometimes you'd see them, rat and roach alike, in the hallways and the stairs. The rats were long, and fierce, and stared at you unafraid, knowing that you—not they—were the intruder, and would, in the end, yield the space.

The roaches, meanwhile, were among the largest you'd ever seen. Huge. Black. Shiny. Like stone scarabs in an Egyptian tomb. They'd crush beneath your heel with a sound like that of a walnut breaking. Or they wouldn't crush at all, which was worse. You'd feel them as tough and hard as a lead fish weight under your sole, then you'd lift your foot, and they'd scurry away, unharmed.

*

More background. There is an awkwardness in your relationship with some of your fellow employees.

Oh, not with the people on your own magazine . . . many of whom are engineers who made the transition to publishing for a variety of obscure reasons, or else they were old school journalists, come to the trade press in search of higher salaries and greater stability than can be got in newspapers. With them, you have a curious bond. They, like you, share a certain sense of being ill at ease, of historical or personal displacement.

But yours was not the only magazine on the floor. There was another magazine. Call it the Other. Where yours was older, and more technical, the Other was new. It covered the use of PCs in large corporations. The management of the company had very high hopes for this publication, thinking of it as Cutting Edge and Exciting.

Its editor is a young man, acerbic, cruelly witty in personal conversation, affecting severe black-framed glasses and British suits, a darling of the corporation. The publisher is a huge, fleshy former jock, a long time employee, who is (at the age of 40-something) married and yet also having an affair with the daughter of a man high up in the company, thus giving him, too, a certain power.

And the rest of the editorial staff is likewise young, likewise ambitious. Likewise . . . different from you.

*

Indeed, while no one will, of course, actually come out and say it, the Other is staffed by aristocrats. They are the children of kings. Or, more precisely, of advertisers.

It is a simple quid pro quo. Controlled circulation, trade-press magazines cannot be published without advertisers to fund them. The advertisers are companies owned or controlled by powerful people. The powerful sometimes have children who wish to get into "the exciting and glamorous field of publishing." Magazines are always in need of editors. So why not arrange a little swap?

*

Now, you took the job on 1 July. By 2 July, you had already discovered that the political situation was complex. Because of the shortage of space, your bosses had put you ("short term") in an office up on the sixth floor, where the managers were. Your arrival had been greeted by the people already there with all the joy which they might express at the appearance of plague bearing vermin. You had discovered that there was an enormous sense of distaste for your magazine among the Powers That Be, who regarded it as old fashioned and your publisher (a grand old man of the industry who'd founded the magazine decades before) as a fossil. You heard comments . . . spoken just loud enough to be certain that you would hear . . . like, "Amazing. Last month we even made money on . . .[insert your publication name here]". There was even speculation that your magazine would be closed down entirely, its resources given to The Other.

You were thus relieved when, some weeks into it, you were moved downstairs to a desk on your magazine's floor, near the fire escape.

The fire escape is important to your story.

And not because of fire.

*

Your son was born in August. Because you still didn't know your co-workers very well, you celebrated by offering them a gift. You brought in honey and imported crackers, and left them near the coffee machines with a note that this was a token of the birth of your son.

You noticed that the Fine Young Editors of the Other consumed your offerings with due speed. But no one appeared at your desk to offer you either thanks or congratulations.

*

You began work at your new desk.

You noticed that there was a smell around the stairs of the fire escape. It was heavy, chemical, and sometimes faintly metallic. You asked your co-workers about it. One of them, a tall lesbian who was the news editor and with whom you had developed a friendship, said that a memo had come around some weeks ago. The building management was spraying in the basement because of rats and roaches. "They're trying to exterminate everything two feet long or above," she said. You laughed.

And you forgot about the issue.

*

Now we come to the interesting part.

It is an early morning. Because of the complexity of the train schedule, you sometimes find it easier to come in at about 8:00. This is, technically, before the opening of the office, though of course the eager beavers of the Other are frequently at their desks before seven.

But today, the building is nearly empty. You are alone at your desk, eating a buttered muffin you'd gotten on the way from the train, and drinking a cup of coffee.

You hear a voice.

It is your boss. "I have a somewhat delicate question," he says.

*

Fifteen minutes later, you are sitting still. You are amazed.

What your boss, your editor in chief, has asked is, "Do you have a personal hygiene problem?"

It seems that someone, he will not say who, but several people, have come to him to complain about your smell. "People have said, 'Boy, that [your name here] sure has a hell of a body odor problem.'"

At first, you think it's a joke. You don't believe it. Then, when you realize he's serious, you are frightened. You explain, weakly, that the odor to which the complaints refer is most likely the smell from the basement. The pesticide.

He says, Oh.

*

You ask the names of your accusers. He will not tell you.

*

You go to your managing editor (ME). You tell him the story. He blanches. (You hear later than he went to the Assistant ME and says, "What is the worst possible thing he [the editor in chief] could do?")

He assures you that your job is safe. He makes discrete inquiries.

Some days later he comes to you and says, sotto voice, that the complaints had come from the Other. The young and talented and well bred over there had complained.

About you.

*

You take some simple countermeasures. At one point, while at the coffee machine where lots of people can hear you, you tell a co-worker that someone . . . ha ha ha . . . had actually believed that the smell of pesticide from the basemen had been . . . ha ha ha . . . you. Wasn't that funny?

And one of the people listening, a woman of the Other, a young person with the pinched face of someone for whom nothing is ever quite satisfactory, says to you, "Oh, so *that's* what it is."

She does not, however, apologize.

*

Frustrated, you make a small gesture. You find an advertisement that shows a cartoon skunk pointing at the viewer over the caption, "The Skunkworks Want You!" You copy and post it beside your desk.

One day the fleshy jock who is the publisher of the Other goes past. You are amused to see him start, almost say something, then with a strangled sound, hurry on.

*

Months pass. Then two years.

You take another job, elsewhere. You do not, however, forget the incident. It isn't easy to forget. At a time when you had been very, very fragile, those of the Other had struck you hard. You carry the bruise.

While you don't often think of it, once in a while you do have a curious fantasy . . . while you sit idle at your desk after filing a long and difficult story . . . a fantasy in which the worst-case scenario had occurred. In the daydream, you had been fired. You had been without a job while your infant son and wounded wife were imprisoned in the heat and the dust of the decaying City of the North.

In your imagination, it becomes a kind of movie. A horror movie. You work on the camera angles. The dialog.

We see you, in the little film, pink slip in one hand, exiting the building with your belongings in a cardboard box. You weep on the bus.

Then, Cut To the shadowy recesses of the Building Basement. There, we see boxes, dirt, the concrete floor, piles of paper and old magazines . . . all in twilight.

In the gloom, we faintly detect something . . .a movement, something curved, small, hard-shelled. We see the spasmodic movement of jointed legs . . .

*

Establishing shot: we are now upstairs. The guard at the desk downstairs is the first to realize that something is wrong. We see him. He is a sullen high school drop out with bad skin who's been given a uniform and gun and told to protect the Golden Others for minimum wage. He chews an enormous wad of pink gum or brown nicotine spit and reads under the counter a magazine that shows men taking blue rubber phalluses up their rectums.

He hears something. He raises his head. There is a sound like a rustling. Like leaves. Like whispers. Like the sheeted dead.

He stands. He approaches the sealed door of the fire escape, which, as it was with yours, is behind his desk. He walks slowly, cautiously, curiously . . . chewing his gum or tobacco with a new intensity, so that his jaw seems almost to be hinged, like an insect's, sideways.

He comes to the door. He puts his hands to it, then leans his ear to the steel, and we hear with him the mysterious rustling now grown enormous, ominous . . .

We tense ourselves, knowing what's coming as he pulls at the handle . . .

SMASH CUT: the space beyond the door, teaming with . . .

Them.

*

Anyone with even a passing familiarity with the conventions of horror films will of course be able to extrapolate from there, as the mutant bugs climb the stairs, burst forth from fire escapes and air vents and ceilings . . . their hunger not sated until they have feasted one and all on human flesh, pink and prime and delivered fresh ground as the camera watches in morbid fascination.

But, there, alas, your imagination fails you. It is beyond the power of your abreaction to go to that logical if gristly conclusion. As much as you might enjoy it, you just can't envision your co-workers turned into so much *Pâté de foie gras.*

So, instead, in your cinematic fantasy, the Bugs do not develop a taste for meat, but they do eat damn near everything else. Up the hallways, the stairways, the walls themselves . . . they crawl in a gray, clicking mass . . . hanging from the ceiling and the windows like enormous rotting grapes or fungus on a tree ... consuming Everything. The stale sandwich crusts left in the lunch room trash cans, the candy bars in office desks, the reporters' note books and the copies current issues, the hanging files, the boxes of copier paper . . . the sweet, dried sugar on the inside of the soda bottles left on desktops ...wall paper paste and the adhesive under the carpet.

And we see the preoccupied editor of the Other. He of the black rims and caustic wit. He is speaking into a phone while staring intently into his screen where a matrix of numbers is displayed on a spreadsheet. He reaches, distracted, for his coffee cup. His lips touch it . . .

And he sees.

It brims with hard gray bodies, legs, eyes.

*

The golden children of the Other run screaming into the street, leaving their cubicles behind.

*

That brings you to the end of your cinematic fantasy. Once or twice, you seriously consider making it into a film script. But nothing comes of it. Just as well. What producer would touch the story?

Besides, as time goes on, there comes to be no need for your revenge, imaginary or otherwise. In hardly more than a year, the publishing company discovers a hard truth—to wit, it cannot make money by publishing magazines about the glamorous uses of computers in Corporate America. It doesn't know how. And perhaps it never will. The company has always made its money from publications in very, very small niches . . . *Decorative Brick Maker Magazine, The Journal of Industrial Feed Processing, Fastener and Seal News* . . . fields so small that there isn't really room for more than one or two magazines, and so there's very little competition.

And a general purpose PC publication at the time of our story does not meet that criteria. Indeed, the Other Magazine faces competitors at every turn . . . competitors with deep pockets, and technical expertise, and what space reps refer to as "Group Buys."

So . . .

*

And it is now several years later.

You are working at a start up magazine. You actually have a very small equity position in it . . . not much. A trifle. Just enough to keep you interested. For awhile.

You are in a distant city. You forget, later, which city it was. There are so many. It is a trade show. You walked the floor of a large auditorium full of computer users and the booths of vendors—Microsoft, IBM, HP, Sun.

And you hear someone say hello. Then tentatively, as though not certain of it, your name.

For a moment, you do not recognize him. You realize, then, that it is the large, fleshy, ex-jock publisher . . . former, you correct yourself . . . former publisher of the defunct Other. Very defunct, you add. Defunct and buried.

You speak to him, warmly. You shake hands. He is delighted to see you again. He questions you . . . where you are, what you are doing. Then, slowly, attempting to be subtle but failing spectacularly, he wonders if you would arrange an introduction to your publisher. He wonders if, as he has heard, there might be openings in sales at your publication.

Ah.

You say, of course, of course, and later arrange a meeting for him.

(He does not get the job.)

*

You will reflect on your emotions about it all. On some level, you are startled by how little you actually feel, the man who had wounded you coming now to you hat in hand. There is no sense of vengeance. You seem to have—surprise—carried no real grudge toward him.

Besides, you are beyond all that. You, the child of Puritans for whom emotion itself, like vanity, was questionable, you would never let yourself go so far as to feel satisfaction at the discomfort of another.

No.

And yet . . .

And yet . . .

On the other hand.

You cannot say you are displeased.

PSI

α. What is this?

So what is this? asks Raziel, Angel of Mysteries, Spirit of Secret Regions, Chief of the Supreme Ambiguities, Personification of Divine Wisdom, and, somewhat improbably (indeed, laughably) presented here as the Voice Of Common Sense.

It is, *answers the author*, an amusing little pastiche or perhaps burlesque… in any case a fiction…presented as a dialog or conversation between the author's pretensions and conceits on one hand and the spirit of rationality on the other.

Raziel: *Me, in other words. And you.*

Precisely.

Raziel: *And this "burlesque" of yours, how does it begin?*

We are in the home office of Our Hero. He is a short, funny little man of the kind who inhabits these sort of tales. He derives his living from, well, call it real estate management—i.e., looking after his aged father's investments. But he is also an avid if amateur writer of fiction.

Raziel: *And right now your funny little man is?*

Entering his office. It is about nine. His wife is out of the house already. She swims at the pool club three days a week. And this is one such day. He, himself, has a moment of spare time. There is nothing of a business or a personal nature that need be done until noon. So, he takes advantage of his privacy to pursue a particular project that he has had in mind for some time.

Raziel: *Can you be more specific?*

Certainly. He begins by setting up (gingerly!) three votive candles…tall things in a glass vases. Two Michael the Archangels, one Mary. He perches them on the edge of his desk and ignites them with a long nosed butane candle lighter.

29

Raziel: *But his office is full of paper and books and other flammables. Surely this is a fire hazard.*

Which is why he is so careful. And why he waited until his wife was out of the house. So no one will know how stupid he's being.

Raziel: *If he knows it is stupid, then why is he doing it?*

Ah, complicated. He wants to a build a wall to product him and his works from...from...

Raziel: *From what?*

Psychic attack.

β. Curses. Hexes. Psionic weapons

Raziel: *Come again?*

Black magic. Curses. Hexes. Psionic weapons of mass destruction.

Raziel: *I...sorry?*

Well, to explain, you have to know that many, many, *many* years ago...when he was still quite young...Our Hero was a graduate student at a certain university. He hoped to obtain a Ph.D. in one of the liberal arts.

Raziel: *And he did not succeed in this quest?*

He most certainly did not. He had several flaws of character and personality that made it difficult for him to, shall we say? Fit in. And, indeed, in some ways, when he was finally (if oh-so-politely) kicked out of the program, it was all for the best. He could not have survived in the modern academy. At least not as the academy has become. With all its fierce and bloody strife, its few full-time educators and many, many administrators, its purges and ideological witch hunts...

Raziel: *So it was all his fault? His failure, I mean?*

Mostly. Almost entirely. He did many stupid things toward the end. So much so that he sometimes wonders if he actually if unconsciously arranged little dramas to get himself removed from program...since he could not simply walk away from it without disappointing his family.

Yet...

Raziel: *Yet?*

Yet, on some level he suspects that he was at least as much sinned against as sinning. Rather by accident, he offended three powerful professors and these went out of their way to make his life miserable. If they had not been so abusive, then perhaps he would have remained in the program, earned his Ph.D., or at least exited from the University with less drama, angst, and chaos.

Raziel: *I see. Very well. Tell me about them. The Three.*

I shall. One after the other.

γ. **Hurling bans like lighting bolts**

Raziel: *Professor One?*

The first professor was an important man. He was director of graduate studies for the department. He was the editor of a prestigious journal. Aspiring academics knew that they must conform to his conceptions of "genuine scholarship" or face eternal damnation…*Ex cathedra*… expelled from the garden, he with the flaming sword… tyrant of the editorial board, hurling bans like lightning bolts.

Raziel: *Describe him physically.*

He was a big man, tall and fat, in his early 60s, came from very old money, and he affected each of the signs and symbols of his profession: the tweed jacket with the leather patches on the sleeves, the pipe (dear God! a Peterson briar), etc. Oh, and one slightly out of character affectation. He sported a *Magnum P.I* mustache grown in the 1970s (perhaps he wooed his wife with it) and kept ever since.

Raziel: *He was a bad teacher?*

Oh, no. Actually, he could be quite good. His undergraduates genuinely profited from his avuncular pomposity. His graduate students, those that he favored, adored him, and he went out of his way to help them.

Raziel: *But not the hero of story?*

Somewhere, somehow along the way, Our Hero offended Professor One. Perhaps it was his informality of writing and expression (both of which the professor detested). Or perhaps it was they had very different approaches to the study of their shared subject matter—Our Hero was a great fan of the *Annales* and of the Neo-Marxists, while the Professor regarded Marc Bloch and Fernand Braudel as hopelessly materialistic, and the Neo-Marxists? Simply not gentlemen.

Or, perhaps, and this is most likely of all, the Professor detected (or thought he detected) a certain disrespect in Our Hero. Actually, truth to be told, Our Hero held the man in genuine esteem. But, there was something about him…Our Hero's body language, the position of his mouth, the micro-expressions on his face… that the Professor found unsettling. Thus, Our Hero became (innocently, unknowingly) a mirror in which the Professor saw his own self-doubts, his own secret and terrible conviction that what he did was without meaning…his suspicion that his students and his peers regarded him as he did himself, i.e., as a banality, a non-entity, a fraud.

δ. **The Smartest Girl In School**

Raziel: *And Professor Two?*

A young woman. Very bright. Recently arrived from a prestigious school in Manhattan. Tenure track. A face that radiated a certain (false) vulnerability. Elfin or fey, I think, are the words we need. Of course her work had a tinge of Third Wave Feminism. A certain hint of anti-maleness. But these are expected in this day and age. The surprise would be if it were otherwise.

Raziel: *You say she is very intelligent?*

Indeed. Gifted, even. Genius level. She already had one book in print. Another was coming. The University had been delighted to get her, and she was already tenure track.

Raziel: *So, she must have been a good teacher, then. A favorite of her students.*

What makes you say that?

Raziel: *Well, if she was so intelligent...*

Ah, but there is the rub. That she was extremely intelligent is undeniably true, but she had not made...may never make ...the transition from being a student to an educator.

Raziel: *There is a difference?*

Oh, yes. You see, the purpose of a student...and particularly a graduate student...is to display how very bright they are. There is a peacock quality to it. The student says, covertly or overtly, See, see! See how well I have learned! See how marvelously I have taken in the information and processed it and made it mine! The professor may be proud of my accomplishments, because they are in fact *his* accomplishments...*her* triumphs. I have consumed their wisdom and become sage in turn.

Raziel: *But an educator?*

At his best, at her best, the professor or teacher is in the business of concealing rather than revealing their intelligence. Their purpose is no longer to display their achievements, but rather to encourage achievement in others. Yes, the professor may stand at a podium, may be (in theory) the center of attention...but the focus of his efforts, the center of her concerns, is now the student. The spotlight must shift from the inner to the outer.

Raziel: *And she could not do this?*

Indeed. She could not manage the transition from pampered favorite to indulgent mentor. She could not be other than The Smartest Girl In School.

Raziel: *And her classes were?*

Appalling. Once (Our Hero remembers) Professor Two was giving a lecture on social movements. She asked the class if anyone knew the origins of "gay liberation." A young Lesbian woman, only recently out of the closet, proud of herself and her culture, raised a hand and said ...instantly, intensely...The Stonewall Riots.

Wrong...came the word from above. Stonewall was *not* the first. The Professor listed a dozen other incidents that came before the riots. It had been, in other words, a setup. The Professor had asked the question knowing that someone would surely say Stonewall, and knowing also that it would give her a chance to show her superiority by providing the "right" answer.

The young Lesbian left that day… lips tight in fury…hatred in her eye. She had learned nothing, other than that it was dangerous to answer a question posed by her professor.

Raziel: *But you have said that Professor Two was active in the plan to remove Our Hero from the University. Why? What had he done to offend her?*

Oh, many things. Again, there were issues of ideology and methodology. Our Hero cited scholars and philosophers of whom Professor Two did not approve. And there personal issues. Clashes of personality.

But…

Raziel: *But?*

But the biggest thing, the most important thing, was that …well, once or twice, by accident, in classes or presentations…Our Hero took the spotlight away from her. Outshone her. And even if only for a moment, this was…

Raziel: *Unforgivable.*

Quite so.

ε. Most insidiously evil

Raziel: *And Professor Three?*

Is the most insidiously evil of the three, and the most inoffensive.

Raziel: *Come again?*

She appeared at first glance to be sage and supportive. She was Our Hero's major professor, and, for the first two years, a real and active friend to him. She approved his dissertation proposal. She thought it was a "good idea." She read chapters from it. She had no objections and, indeed, praised it highly

Raziel: *But?*

But Professors One and Two became involved as readers. And both of them, for their own reasons (as we have already seen), detested Our Hero and his work.

Raziel: *And then?*

And then it all went wrong. Professors One and Two demanded revision after revision…rejected his every word and phrasing…insisted (insultingly, disgustedly) on rewrite after rewrite.

Raziel: *And she?*

Professor Three…before so much his supporter…announced that, yes, Yes, YES, his dissertation was trash. That it had "no theoretical interpretative apparatus." That he, himself, should ask if he genuinely had a future in the academy.

Raziel: *She betrayed him? Why?*

Because it was easier. They were more forceful than she. More energetic. The man was her boss. The woman, though technically her subordinate, had more impressive credentials and her future was obviously bright. Rather than take arms against these two, it was easier...easier by far...to throw her offending student under the proverbial bus.

Raziel: *Most unpleasant.*

Indeed. Our Hero once wrote a (rather bad) poem about her. In it, he compared her to a jellyfish. Spineless, invertebrate, yet toxic...deadly. She was, he said, like a box jelly or a man o' war. Washed ashore upon a beach. Drying and dying in the sand. Yet still capable of causing harm.

He ended the poem with a vision of a child, barefoot, running in the surf, running on the shore, laughing...

The bare feet coming down upon the gelatinous thing concealed in the sand.

ζ. "A theoretical interpretative apparatus"

Raziel: *But the dissertation? Did he ever complete it?*

Several times over. But it was never accepted. Our Hero wrote and rewrote and rewrote his dissertation...time and time and time again. He tried his best (he really did) to meet their constantly shifting requirements... their contradictory diktats, their non-negotiable demands that shifted and changed from moment to moment...

Raziel: *They intended to never allow him graduate. They intended to torture him in this way. Until finally he left so they didn't have to throw him out.*

Yes, though it is not clear he understood that fact. He is, alas, in his way, not terribly bright. And so he thought that maybe, maybe there was still a chance they would allow him to graduate. So...he rewrote the dissertation one last time, and this time selected as his "theoretical interpretative apparatus" a hodgepodge of ideas picked up from medical anthropology.

Strangely, his conscious mind thought it was a good idea. He thought maybe they would finally accept it. Hadn't they been asking for theory all along? Was this not a complex, well-defined, applicable interpretive device?

But...

Surely, he knew on some level that it was not so. Surely he must have known, deep down, they would reject it. So, perhaps, his final rewrite was simply yet another unconscious gesture...a kind of academic suicide. For, of course, they despised it. And the registered letter saying that they would no longer work with him arrived two weeks later.

And that was the end of it.

η. A venomous slime

Raziel: *But the candles? What has this all to do with the candles?*

Ah, the votive candles. Yes.

Well, you will remember that I said that Our Hero is an amateur (if not particularly talented) writer. He has, over the decades that separate him from his debacle in graduate school attempted several short stories and a novel or two that incorporated the Three as characters.

Raziel: *Such as?*

Well, first there was a horror novel he began way, way back. In it the Three are professors at a certain unnamed university. A demon visits and tempts each with everything their desire. They each, in turn, accept the bargain. The price is, however, that during the full moon they take on the forms of the creatures they most resemble—Professor One, a ravenous beast that consumes human flesh; Professor Two, a giant leach that lives on blood; Professor Three, a venomous slime.

For a time, in these forms, they bring a reign of terror to the little industrial city where-in may be found their university. But, then, the hero of the piece—a young woman based on a graduate student that Our Hero really knew at the time—obtains the aid of angels and destroys them one by one.

Raziel: *Did he ever publish this book? This horror novel?*

No. And that was the curious thing. He never even finished it. Mid-way through, at the worst possible moment, when he had already completed so much and only needed to push on for a few final months of work…he lost interest in it. He simply could not find the energy to proceed. And so the novel, half written, languished on his disk drive.

θ. The demon was a nice guy

Raziel: *He never did anything more with this horror novel of his?*

Well, sort of. A few years ago, he thought he might salvage something of his work. So, he picked up the unfinished narrative and attempted to incorporate certain of its elements into yet another book, this time a comic meta-fictive novel involving a writer who is approached by one his characters—it is, in fact, the demon from the horror novel mentioned above. The demon then attempts to persuade the author to finish the work so that he, the demon, can achieve completeness. However, we learn that the demon (who is actually a rather nice guy, "I'm not bad. I'm just written that way.") is secretly in love with the main character, the young woman, and his real purpose is to make certain that *she* comes into being. In the end of the book, they marry and live happily (if virtually) ever after.

Raziel: *Sounds intriguing. Did he finish that one?*

Yes…but also no. He wrote it, but on re-reading decided it was just no damn good. So he rewrote it. And it wasn't much better. So he tried again. Still no improvement. And so on.

Raziel: *Is this normal for him?*

No. That was the curious thing. He is not a terrific writer. He is no genius. But it is rare for him to write quite as badly as he did on these occasions. In fact, he found it quite disturbing. There was something almost eerie about it. It was as though each time he tried to write about The Three, his (admittedly limited) talents abandoned him.

Raziel: *Disconcerting.*

To say the least.

ι. A Plague of boils

Raziel: *And has he tried to write about them again since then?*

Twice. In fact, just this month and last. He recently tried a new kind of writing, one that combined certain elements of the fantastic with extreme realism. In the process, he did two very long novellas roughly based on the life of a friend of his and on his own experience with the academy. In the stories, the Three appeared as his friend's tormentors, but then they are given their just desserts though a combination of real world circumstances (they are removed from their teaching positions) and purest fantasy (they encounter spirits and angels).

Raziel: *And were these novellas better than the books he'd attempted?*

Maybe a little. But the really interesting thing was physical and biological rather than aesthetic. You see, he finished the first novella on a Thursday. The following morning he began vomiting. Or, rather, not just vomiting, but turning his guts inside out. It was (I think) what they call "projectile vomiting," interspaced with episodes of explosive diarrhea. And, late in the afternoon, when there was nothing in him any longer, long and painful periods of dry heaves.

Raziel: *Unpleasant. Food poisoning? Or a virus?*

He never knew. One or the other. But he was better by Saturday and he assumed the incident was over. He set to work, then, and over the next few days worked on the second novella that referenced The Three. Again, he finished on a Thursday.

Raziel: *And on Friday morning?*

Found he was running a temperature of 103.8 F. He slept most of that day, and then on Saturday realized that he also a painful rash on his feet and hands. He went to "urgent care" (a misnomer if there ever was one) on Sunday. There he learned he had "Food, Hand, And Mouth Disease." This is a common illness among children and infants, and when children and infants get it, the symptoms are usually quite mild.

But when an adult gets it…well, it can be, sometimes, rather awful.

And that's what he had. The next few weeks were singularly unpleasant—blisters and boils on his hands and feet, shedding skin like a snake, having toe nails come loose and fall away.

Not fun at all.

κ. As if he were cursed

Raziel: *As if he were cursed.*

Yes. He begins to wonder if, could it be, just maybe there's some bizarre link between his writing about the Three and his back luck? A hex, if you will?

Could it even be, he wonders, that somehow The Three have a supernatural power? The ability to sense when someone is writing unflattering things about them? And to project malevolent thoughts in the direction of the offender? Sort of like the characters in the book *Conjure Wife*. A comparison all the more apt given that it is a university setting…

λ. Psionic laser

Raziel: *But he is a rationalist, or tries to be. Surely he doesn't believe such twaddle.*

You are correct. He does *not* really believe it. Not deep down.

But there is a part of him that… wonders. It speculates. It provides a pseudo-rational justification for his concern. He was a great reader of science fiction as a boy, and in SF there have always been stories of ESP and the paranormal, of telepathy and psychic powers, of Psi and Psionics.

And, really, is it so absurd to suspect such things might really exist? That maybe, somehow, there is an undetected segment of the electro-magnetic spectrum? And that, maybe, certain people have sections of the brain modified or mutated to allow them to perceive (however dimly) that otherwise invisible form of radiant energy?

More, if any of that were true, might it not be possible as well for such people to collect and focus such energies in a coherent beam? To direct those energies (laser-like) towards a target?

To, in other words, bless or curse?

Raziel: *Our Hero suspects then if he has been hexed by the Diabolic Three?*

Precisely. He wonders if they have somehow sensed a Disturbance In The Force. Then, consciously or unconsciously, they have responded psychically. First they made him lose interest in the horror novel. Then they made his meta-fiction wretched. Then, when he still didn't get the message, they made him ill. If he continues, heaven only knows what will occur. Death and destruction, perhaps. Or plagues of locusts. Why not? He's already had the plague of boils.

μ. Psychic amplifier

Raziel: *So the candles...?*

Well, remember, Our Hero doesn't *really* believe any of this. But...but...it can't hurt to sort of take a few counter measures. Just in case. So, maybe...he thinks...he could construct a kind of psychic wall...a block...a psionic warfare countermeasure...that will at least keep their lethal emanations at bay.

Raziel: *And he does this... how?*

He hopes that he has some small psychic capacity in his own right. And, maybe, he may amplify what little he has via artificial means. After all, there is precedent. Does not religion seem to form a sort of psychic amplifier? Are there are not studies that reveal that those who have strong belief systems are healthier and stronger, and more able to rebound from adversity, than those who do not possess such armor?

Raziel: *So, what measures does he take? How does he attempt to strengthen his latent or limited powers of psychic defense?*

Oh, rituals, rites, symbols and so on. This story, for one thing, which he writes to focus his energies. And it isn't that bad an idea, really. His most important *intellectual* passion (as opposed to other kinds) is his writing, at which he may not be good but about which he is fervent. Ergo, if there is anything to his theory of latent or micro psychic powers of the brain, then this ...the story, the narrative...may be the best way to invoke them.

Then, too, he employs various rituals and emblems to stimulate the neurons of Psi and telepathic shields— thus he searches the web for protective images: the *Sigillum Dei Aemeth* and John Dee's *Monas Hieroglyphica*... He rereads Gustav Davidson's *A Dictionary of Angels* for prayers and spells and invocations—viz., the "conjuration of the sixth mystery with the seal of the power-angels," and "conjuration of the sword" (pages 357 and 358 respectively).

Raziel: *And, of course, there is me.*

Exactly. Raziel. Page 242 in Davidson. Personification of the divine wisdom. "...author of *The Book of the Angel Raziel* ...'where-in all celestial and earthly knowledge is set down.'"

η. Votives

Raziel: *You still have not yet explained the candles.*

Oh. Yes. The candles. Which are somewhat ironic since he isn't even Catholic. But, he and his wife got them when they first moved into the new house. They had a fireplace but for a variety of safety reasons they didn't want to burn wood in it. So, they got candles instead...votive ones, because they were cheapest...and used those to create the illusion of an open fire. It was quite comfortable, really. But then they got a gas log insert instead and the candles have simply sat unused on the hearth.

Raziel: *Until—let me guess— he remembered them.*

Quite so. Precisely so. He added them to the whole little spectacle as yet another invocation of the divine. Though, come to think of it, his purposes might have better served with candles devoted to less orthodox figures. Perhaps he should have purchased (and he has seen them in stores) candles for Santa Muerte. Since curses are involved.

Raziel: *Or even for H.P. Lovecraft's Cthulhu. If you're looking for supernatural drama.*

Not a bad idea at all. But he does not know where to buy them.

Raziel: *Sure to be on the net, somewhere.*

n. Candles, chants, images

Raziel: *We may assume that he now performs his rite, his magic incantation, his psychic exercise, his psionic meditation.*

Quite so. He lights the candles. He chants. He contemplates the mystic images. He makes mesmeric passages with wand and hand. He turns to his laptop and writes this story in a single sitting.

Raziel: *Does it work? I mean, does his little experiment with magic improve his luck, ward off the curse, whatever?*

Apparently not. His father…his aged father…has (had) two dogs who are (were) dear to him. The day after he finishes his rite and writing, one of the two dogs must be put down. It is very sad and very unexpected. On Sunday, the animal was fine and happy and playing energetically with the children from across the way. On Tuesday, he was dying. He was gone.

Raziel: *Sad.*

Very.

Raziel: *So if there really is a curse, then Our Hero's attempts at blocking it have failed.*

It would seem so.

ξ. They are useless

Raziel: *If that is the case, does that mean that Our Hero will give in to the inevitable? Will he cease writing about the Three out of fear of their malevolent sorcery?*

Yes and no.

Raziel: *Another puzzle. Speak plainly, I beg you.*

He will never write again about The Three. Not even once. He will, in fact, go back into some of the other stories he's written and remove references to them. But this is not …repeat, not…because he fears them.

Raziel: *Then why?*

Because they bore him.

Raziel: *Clarify*.

Upon long reflection, he has realized they just aren't really all that interesting as people. Which makes them useless as models for fictional characters.

0. Surely they would inspire

Raziel: *Pardon me? How is that possible? Does he not hate them? Surely they would inspire excellent villains for his works.*

You would think so, wouldn't you? But, in fact, they fail as villains. Oh, yes, they are mean in their petty little way. And they have caused him harm (even if he acknowledges his own share of blame in that). But, let us face it, a good villain is a little over the top, a little camp, has a touch of Dr. No and Blofeld. And they have nothing of that sort. They are bland. They have no melodrama, no energy, no pyrotechnics. At best, they are like the damned in *Screwtape Letters*. Just self-conscious enough to know that they are doing evil (and thus to be damned), but not so much as to risk becoming at the last moment a saint.

π. "Beautiful but without peace"

Raziel: *Well, all right. But they have still provided him with strong emotions. Surely, then, his distaste could be converted to admiration. Could they not, therefore, be turned into heroes? Surely they could be ...ah...wise professors defending the Life Of The Intellect from the barbarism of the age. From, in effect, the author of this very tale?*

Again, you would think so, but no. They are equally useless as literary heroes, and for rather similar reasons. I believe it was Bismarck who said the quality of greatness has in it a touch of the Fallen Angel, "beautiful but without peace." This is true, and I think it is true because the genuine hero must attempt a task so vast, battle an evil so monstrous, that he or she is bound to fail, at least to some degree. (The triumph, no matter how brilliant, is always partial.) The real act of heroism, the genuine grandeur, is not in the success of the venture but rather in the enormity of the challenge. It comes when the protagonist stands at the edge of void...before the dragon, Tiamat, Leviathan...and proclaims unashamedly "in spite of all appearances to the contrary, I am your worthy adversary." And they, The Three, are nothing like that. They issue no challenges to infinity. Their goals are reasonable and rational and quite easily obtainable—to wit, dominance in their tiny niches of specialization, the humiliation of their professional enemies, the occasional destruction of a recalcitrant student.

ρ. Kafka's Cockroach

Raziel: *Ah. All right. But there is yet another great character to be found in fiction. There is the man or woman of pathos. The man or woman with whom we may identify…in spite of, or because of their failings. The man or women in whom we may see ourselves because we recognize in their meaningless existence our own equal insignificance. Even Kafka's cockroach has a claim on our affections. Surely The Three can have no less appeal.*

Alas. Alas. Once more, no. They will never be fodder for the next Edward Albee. They will never inspire another *Who's Afraid Of Virginia Woolf.* To be pathetic you must have the quality of almost being successful. You must have the knowledge that if only, if only, things had been a little different…if only you'd gotten the breaks…you would have been a titan. But not the Three. They have no real capacity for greatness. Large as they may loom in their own minds, they are limited people. They have not the option of being more than they are. They have always been, will always be (to paraphrase John Fowles) grotesquely elongated shadows…monstrous dwarfs.

Raziel: *So, not being inspired, the Three inspire nothing?*

Precisely so. Which is why Our Hero will never write of them again.

σ. Dismissing the writer

Raziel: *And that is the end?*

Quite so. He is done. Our Hero has finished his efforts. He saves his file. Blows out the candles. Puts them away. Gets on with his life.

Raziel: *So you have finished your story.*

Why, so I have.

Raziel: *And a job well done, I might add.*

Really? You are too kind.

Raziel: *In fact, I think, you should now reward yourself. Take a break. Get a cup of coffee. Indeed, why don't you step out for a bit. Head up to the Starbucks on Tramway and Academy. Get a latte. Or maybe an iced Americano. You deserve it.*

I…I suppose I do. I've worked long and hard today, haven't I? It isn't often I finish a piece in a single sitting.

Raziel: *Exactly. Now, hurry along before you get all guilt-ridden and decide to stay here. Chop chop. Vámonos. Peddle to the metal.*

Right. Right. I'm off. See you in an hour or so.

Raziel: *Ciao. Enjoy.*

[We hear the sound of retreating steps. The front door closes and is locked from outside. We hear the author's little truck's engine turn over. Then he is gone.]

Raziel: (Turning to Reader) *And now we may chat, yes?*

τ. The Logical Climax

The Reader: (Puzzled. Curious.) Why did you dismiss him?

Raziel: (Who will be henceforth identified only by the fact that his comments are in italics) *I thought we ought to have some time together…without him. You see, he has left out the ending of his tale.*

The Reader: Ah. I wondered. The story seemed to end on a distinct note of anti-climax.

You are perceptive. Yes. He did not provide the necessary culmination…partly because he is not sufficiently discerning to realize that he left something out…but also because he has insufficient courage to follow his fiction to its logical (albeit, irrational and bloody-minded) conclusion.

The Reader: And what is that conclusion? To what end does the premise (inevitably) take us?

What happens is as follows:

Our Hero constructs his reflective psionic screen against the hard magicks of The Three. But, there's the rub. He is not alone. The Three have harmed many, many people over the course of years. They are therefore rich in enemies. There is an endless stream of them —students they have bullied, colleagues whose careers they have blighted, family members they have betrayed or offended.

The Reader: And if Our Hero attempts to construct a shield against the toxic psychic emanations of the Three…?

Then those others do so as well. Indeed, by some mysterious process, traveling along the underground passages of the universal shared unconscious and/or Id, the idea of taking psychic countermeasures leaps from one mind to another…from Our Hero to some other victim of The Three…then to another…and onward and onward.

Soon, all of them, all the wounded and the offended, consciously or unconsciously, begin to construct defenses. They, too, light candles, chant, invoke angels.

The Reader: And soon they are united.

Like a thousand mirrors in the noonday sun. Individually, they may be feeble. Individually, they may reflect only a tiny percentage of the evil of The Three (which is why Our Hero's own shield seems ineffective). But collectively they are titanic. They focus their energies on the squat, ugly, and ill-maintained building which houses the Department.

υ. A Kind of Ritual Sacrifice

The Reader: If it pleases you, present the scene.

It does. I will. It is night. They are the only ones in the building. They are meeting in the big conference room on the top floor to discuss the new graduate students, the incoming class. Or more precisely, they are deciding which one they will destroy. Who they will select to be the semester's pariah…. whose life they will damage and whose aspirations they will blast and wither…who will be the object lesson, a warning to the others, keep them in line …a kind of ritual sacrifice without the sanction of the blade.

And just as they have made their decision, selected a name and a victim, the floor begins to shake...

φ. Meteors fall from heaven

The Reader: And then?

Earthquakes. Tidal Waves. Meteors fall from heaven.

The Reader: A micro-apocalypse...

There is news coverage. There are photos from helicopters and drones. A vast sinkhole, perfectly circular, has formed at the University...directly under the Department and its dingy building...

The video from the drones (in the moments before they vanish mysteriously) reveals sulfuric fires deep, deep within the chasm. In the flames are dancing figures, seen only in silhouette, horned and clawed, and one may distinctly hear the strains of Night On Bald Mountain.

The Reader: And in the morning?

The police, the National Guard, firemen, rescue services, first responders, they are on the scene. They find, by first light, that there have been additional quakes...aftershocks...during the night. The sinkhole has collapsed upon itself. Nothing now confronts them but ruins and rubble. There is no sign of the dancing figures, though there is a lingering odor of sulfur, and some very sensitive souls claim that they can hear, faintly, the strains of Mussorgsky emanating from the ground for some weeks to come.

The Reader: Are there casualties. Many dead?

The curious thing is...no. When all the counting's done, when the noses are tallied and the names taken, it is discovered that while the building is gone, and the whole east end of the University is no more, no one seems to have died. There are no bodies discovered in the rubble. All the students are accounted for. The faculty and administrators were at home. The cleaning crew was on break. Everyone was somewhere else that night.

Except...

The Reader: Except, obviously.

The Three.

The Reader: Not that I am surprised, of course. And even about them about them there is some question. Their bodies are never recovered. They are simply missing in action.

Exactly. Though we may assume that they now dance for all eternity with the horned things, the imps, the fiends, the talon'd harpies, the beasts of the sinkhole.

χ. Malice. Magic.

The Reader: I'm curious. Is the author...Our Hero...aware of any of this? Does he know the end of the story he has created?

No. As I say, he is ignorant. He is innocent (in a manner of speaking). He has simply failed to follow the inner logic of his tale to its inevitable conclusion. Fiction operates under a logic of its own, and a logic which requires conclusions that may not be rational (may not, that is, be governed by the underlying principles of the material universe) but which are inescapable. Every story is its own universe, has its own physics, its own inevitabilities.

The Reader: Should we tell him? Enlighten him?

No. He would not understand. Would lack the courage to understand. The toughness to accept the end.

The Reader: True of more Creators than you would think.

As is for the best. Otherwise…40 days. Forty nights.

The Reader: But surely there is some reason to tell this tale. Surely there is something to learn from it.

You wish instruction from the story? A wisdom to be derived?

The Reader: Yes. If it wouldn't be too much trouble.

Very well. We may explicate the text:

First, you must understand that Our Hero is the not really our hero. He is not the main character. Or rather, not the only main character. He shares the stage (and flaws) of The Three.

The Reader: I see. And his magic? His experiments with psionic technology?

Also less important than you might think. You see, in this story, magic serves only an allegorical purpose. It is appears on stage wearing a great sign that reads, "I am a metaphor. I am a symbol."

The Reader: Ah, indeed? A metaphor, then, for what? A sign of which meaning? Pray, explain your semiotics.

Magic, here, or, if you like, Psi, stands in for unreason. For, that is, hated. Theirs for him, but also his for them. Neither is without sin in that regard.

The Reader: Of course. I see. Quite so. Continue.

And we must understand, magic…in its imaginary world…and malice…in the material…are very much alike. Both have unintended but inescapable consequences.

Thus, in narrative, in Our Hero's story…and in tales like it…when you first draw pentagrams, light candles white and dark…evoke spirits of the moon…you inevitably open doors you later wish you had not. You summon fiends. That is the underlying logic of the fiction of curses and hexes.

The Reader: And in the real world?

In the real world… cruelty. Spite. Vindictiveness. Hatred. Whatever you elect to call it, it is dangerous. No matter how petty, no matter how much you pretend it is justified, no matter how much you rationalize it as "intellectual rigor" or "professionalism" or "genuine scholarship" … ultimately, ultimately, in one way or another…it consumes you. It takes from you your talents and your promise and all your might-have-beens.

For example, in the case of Our Hero, it stripped him of what little creativity he has (and he has so little to spare). In his furious passion he could not portray The Three as people. They became instead mere caricatures…as marionettes whose sole purpose was to goosestep unwaveringly to the Sinkhole, and then to fall, with ear-piercing (if unconvincing) shrieks to their damnation.

The Reader: And what of The Three? What of their hatreds?

For them, who can say? But, perhaps it will be worse. Worse even than the death of the capacity of creation. Because, Our Hero's tale did convey one small truth. The Three have hurt a great many people in the past. They are hurting more now. They do so because they think that it is inevitable. Because that is the way the game is played. Because that's how you get a reputation. Because that is how you keep people (your students) in line.

But …but…there is a problem with this strategy. This plan for life. You make foes of those who might have been friends, or even just neutrals. And, you awaken one day to find you have filled your world with rancor. With enmity. With rage.

And that is not happy world in which to dwell.

But, by then, you cannot escape it. Too many of your victims dream of your discomfiture. Even of your demise.

ψ. The Moral

The Reader: So the moral of the story is…

It is banal. It is clichéd. It is hackneyed.

The Reader: But it is true. Therefore speak it.

I shall. It is…

Avoid. Avoid. Enter not the Demon Haunted Darkness.

Or it will, in the end, devour you. Utterly. And not even bones, blackened and charred, will remain as evidence…

That you ever lived at all.

ω

WALRUS

It all seems so very, very far away, now. Before his death. There in the sixth floor office where the Up And Coming had their fortress . . . though it was three floors and an infinity removed from the office of the Great Old One and thus from genuine power.

It was the very early 1980s. You had somehow become a low-level editor with a trade press publication. You worked on articles about alphanumeric terminals.

That alone should inform the reader how long ago and far away this story truly is.

*

You were very young. And the company had its own building downtown. It was a great, box-like thing squeezed into a space somewhere between the Freeway and the Pru. It was painfully over-crowded. There were magazines and newsletters and directories on every floor.

For that reason, when you report for your first day of work, your bosses explain that, in the very short run, they will be putting you upstairs. At a desk that just happens to be available on the sixth floor.

And so, your managing editor, a great heavy man who has been in the industry forever and bears an eerie resemblance to Lou Grant from the old TV show, has taken you in tow upstairs and directed you to your new desk. He also introduces you to Katie, the (somewhat fluttery) young woman who is the receptionist and provides clerical support to the Managers.

And there, you soon discover, you are the only editorial staff member on a floor otherwise reserved for the best and the brightest.

And they detest you.

*

It was all politics, of course. Before your time, in the long years after the war, the trade press in general, and the company in particular, had been run by salesmen. Great beefy Willy Lomans who affected cigars the size of bus mufflers and drank scotch neat and reminisced wistfully about the times when they, then young, had come ashore with flame throwers and what the Japs in the bunkers looked like afterwards. These were the men of the Trade Press. The Niche Press. The men who founded the industry trade rags about car parts or false teeth or adhesives or, well, whatever, and sold the ads, and hired the editors and dealt with printers and got little black cancers on their foreheads because of the hours they'd spend driving to visit their clients, in the days before telemarketing, and the sun burned through the un-tinted auto glass and their skin bubbled like old paint blistering with the passage of years.

The president of your company is one of these. A gigantic brown dwarf of a man who smelled of El Perfectos and spewed when he ate and told off color jokes . . . and who, you found, you rather admired. He'd come back from Normandy with one hand as a hook and built an empire of niche publications. And now, he, The President, sat immobile and immense in an enormous office that occupied nearly a fourth of floor nine. People called him The Great Old One. Perhaps in reference to H.P. Lovecraft. But probably not.

However, some years before, in the changing world of media conglomerates and global multinationals, he'd sold the firm to a British corporation which in turn had marketed itself to a Dutch giant, and now a new class of manager has come to take command.

*

You rarely deal with the other inhabitants of the sixth floor. There are several severe young men and women—apparently identical, in white or blue shirts, red and yellow power ties, the colors of coral snakes. But, in transit, from men's room to lunch, in conversations staged for your consumption, the petty bullying of office life…you hear them discuss your publication.

They long for its destruction.

*

And on the floor, some clearly have more clout than others.

There is a man who hurries in and out. He is middle-aged. Heavy paunch. Gray of skin yet energetic. He has a great mustache. You come to think of him, later, after he has begun to hate you, as the Walrus. He is powerful. You never bother to learn his exact position. Suffice that he more than anyone will directly determine the fates of publications here. Severe young men and women bring him spreadsheets and proposals. He gazes at the papers and printouts intently. He dispenses cryptic comments . . . "the numbers don't make sense," "cut the fat," "re-position" . . . and then (magically, mysteriously) people are without jobs. He is feared, naturally, but not by the severe young men and women in power ties who surround him. He is older than they by a decade or so. But he is their leader. The older brother in the battle with Father. Against the Great Old One.

He is rumored to have a lover among the severe young women, something you discover much later through gossip at the water cooler. You admit to being amazed. In the current age of suit and counter-suit, what fool in his (or her) right mind would sleep with a co-worker? A subordinate at that?

"Well," says the executive editor, "I'll tell you a story. Once upon a time . . ." he, the executive editor, had been returning from a trade show in a Great Southern City. In that day, the Southern City's airport had been huge, the different terminals linked by a small, automated train.

On the train as the executive editor had been making his way to his plane, he'd looked up and . . . behold! . . . there was the Walrus, heading for the same plane. Except, "he was drunk as a skunk. I mean, *plastered*. Pee-Elll-Ass-Turd." And he had on one side of him a call girl, and another on the other. He'd fall to the left, and the prostitute on that side would push him back up. Then he'd fall to the right, and the other one would catch him there. The last he, the executive editor, saw of the man, the two women were steadying him as he vomited lustily into a trashcan outside security.

*

Now, Katie.

Not a big part of the story, but she plays her role. Because she alone will talk to you there on the sixth floor, you develop…if not exactly a friendship …then at least an acquaintanceship with her. You talk. You speak. You sometimes linger by her desk. She is your only human contact, there. No one else will make conversation.

She is smallish. Flirtatious. Pretty, at least in the passing way of extreme youth . . . prettiness which is not lasting beauty, and which will in the end give way to fat and the generic melon-brained vacuity of a certain sort of suburban life.

You meet her once at the Arlington Street subway stop and walk with her to the company offices. She bounces into your arm and apologizes. You make light of it. Not at all, you say. You enjoyed it, you add.

"You're married," she says. Spoken as a hunter would address a deer head. Already on a wall.

*

And Katie has bought power.

Not that she possesses power. Rather, she has internalized the White Collar Civilization's conception of the universe . . . its unspoken rankings, hierarchies, licenses…

And all this you discover on the unfortunate, final morning.

*

You are working at the desk. You hear a conversation through the open door.

You look up. It is the Walrus. He is speaking to Katie. He is telling her that you…you will have to go. The office here has been claimed by another. She says But what about…? Meaning you. He has to go, he says.

You smile. He sees you. You laugh. You make a joke. You should never make a joke. You realize later that humor, truth expressed in reverse, irony, subtext, these are not just unwelcome. They are deadly. They are suicidal. For they do not recognize power.

And thus it is stupid when you say… with a laugh … well, you've been told to hold the fort and put out landmines and barbed wire.

*

He is standing before you. He is bellowing. He is screaming. He is red in the face and his mustache moves up and down spasmodically, like the hysterically flapping wings of a frightened bat. The faces of severe young men in white shirts are peaking around corners and Katie is watching with her eyes huge and round and her hands over her mouth.

You watch his fury, looking to see if there is foam at his lip

*

By the time you return from lunch, you have been moved. You are downstairs in a makeshift office that was, at one time, a broad space in a hall near the fire escape.

*

It is Katie who explains it to you. Not meaning to. She, in her shallow, unreflective, animal way, she understands what you do not. She says, when she meets you walking one morning from the T-stop. She says, without preamble, without warning, without your raising the subject or saying more than Good-Morning-How-Are-You-Today? Isn't-The-Weather-Lovely? She says, genuinely distressed, genuinely trying to explain, "I'm sorry . . . but my boss is just more important than yours."

And you look at her, startled. For a moment, you are angered. Who gives a flying fuck at a rolling donut whose boss can beat whose and with what hand tied behind their back? But then, the fantastic Absurdity and enormous Truth (both at the same time) of the comment overwhelms your fury. You slide instead into sociological reflections.

Of Course.

For the reality is that organizational behavior is not that far from the school yard...and it takes a child to see that, to see what an adult cannot...that the pimple-faced bully, a cigarette stuffed in his soft half-formed face, leering on the corner at the children smaller than himself, taking their lunch money for the pleasure of being able to do it...

This is the world.

And the rationalist, the adult, the person guilty of maturity until proven innocent...he is a cripple. He cannot understand the motivations, nor predict behaviors of his co-workers.

It is all made clear.

*

Time passes. The Great Old One, upstairs, dies. Your own publisher is eased out. There is some kind of confusion regarding Katie and she moves to California.

You remain at the company for roughly a year longer—you know, of course, that staying longer is not an option. Not with the sort of enemy you've created for yourself in the form of the Walrus...who continues, by the way, to rise effortlessly in the organizational structure. You hear, finally that he has been named to the company board.

You take another job at another magazine. You write about UNIX, PICK OS, THEOS, computer operating systems of the late '70s and early to mid-80s. From there, you will drift to relational databases. Then technical workstations. And so on. One micro-niche technology specialty to another. It is the key to the trade press journalist's career.

And occasionally, you hear stories of the Walrus.

He marries. He divorces. He re-marries. He divorces again. He lives with a younger woman. She leaves him. He marries a third time. She becomes a devotee of curious religions and faddish Yoga practices and has something to do with UFOs. She takes up residence at an Ashram near Santa Fe. He sees her now and then. He continues his career. He takes the office of the Great Old One.

*

You read the obit in the Globe.

How does he die? Well, take your pick. There are so many options. Perhaps it was a bullet fired by furious pimp in a hotel room in New Orleans one dark Saturday night when the man came to collect his $1000-a-night employee and found her bleeding from the rectum. Maybe he was in a small plane over the Gulf of Maine, on his way to the meeting of the Concerned Directors of Something Or Other, and a storm comes up mysteriously, and the plane vanishes from the radar screen and there is no wreckage leading to speculation that he is still alive somewhere, maybe Argentina, hiding from gambling debts.

Or, more likely still, he simply croaks. The life he's led—the nicotine, the alcohol, the drugs during the '70s, the cocaine in the '80s, the ecstasy in the '90s, the scotch whiskey all the time, the lack of sleep, the weight gained and then lost all in a rush at fat farms, the all-nighters, the Red Eyes, the stale air of sick buildings, the expense account meals, Katie stretched out below his nude and sweating bulk, as he enters her brutally and she squeaks in pain and terror...

And somehow, somewhere, at some moment as he peers deeply into a computer screen and proofs a memo or finds fault in a spreadsheet...

He falls forward. Face into the keys. A line of Hs spirals off to infinity.

Which is, you know, the moral of the story you tell.

That triumph is not necessarily a survival characteristic.

*

And you see the building where you used to work one last time. It is perhaps ten years later. You are downtown on a mission of some sort. Perhaps a press conference to attend. Perhaps an errand. You have gone into a coffee shop afterwards. You are ordering French Roast from the tall thin friendly man behind the desk when you hear a roar and rumble. You say what's that. He says I don't know.

You go outside with your coffee in a paper cup. There is a cloud of dust. You realize it is the old building, that heavy machinery . . . tractors, backhoes, close in on the pile of concrete and stone that were its bones. You learn later than the building had been sold years ago. New owners had decreed its destruction... and quickly!... before someone could discover an historical or aesthetic value to the place, and so frustrate their plans for condos or an office tower.

You watch. A dust cloud rises to the sky. You see it approach. You become uneasy, thinking of asbestos, silica, mold...

So, you turn and flee. Seek safer ground. Your coffee in one hand, your briefcase in the other.

Strangely, it never once occurs to you to look back.

WHEN SHE IS AN OLD WOMAN

1.
It must have been over twenty years ago, now.
And she is surely dead.

2.
What follows will be somewhat complex…at least structurally and to some degree conceptually. It is also transgressive. I will say things that cannot be said. You should, therefore, exercise caution.

3.
The overview: The first section his piece will be a typical (albeit largely plotless) fiction. For its central character, known as "he," the story will have a trade press journalist who is obviously and unoriginally based upon the author. Further, it will have as the main character's antithesis an unpleasant old woman who shall be…in the most polite possible way…abusive to him.

An aside: there will be a note of some comedy here in that the story will involve the main character's inability to tie a tie…that is, to wear successfully the uniform of the American male. The reader might, or might not, see this as an opportunity for a sort of low or "Dutch" clowning.

But, after that, the author will attempt something quite dramatic and perhaps impossible. He will attempt to shift from "fiction" to something more like an essay using the Old Woman as a symbol for a larger issue which at least the author believes to be a genuine (and perhaps deadly) problem within the larger discourse of the West. (It also here that the author becomes genuinely transgressive.)

Will the author be successful in this transition? Well, for that, we can only wait and see.

4.

It begins with *him*, the main character.

He was working then at *Datamation* magazine, which was in those days quite a respectable trade journal in the computer field. He and his colleagues wrote mostly about the men and women who ran the IT departments of bigger companies. It is still with us, actually. I mean, *Datamation*. As of the time I write this (October 2014) it is an online publication owned by QuinStreet Inc. It is rather a good pub, in my humble opinion. I read it now and then. If only to remind myself of my past and my youth.

But, when he was an associate editor there, it was owned by Cahners Publishing and it was based in the little city of Newton, just outside of Boston. Specifically, it was in what was then called the Cahners Building (it has another name now, I believe) and which was then and probably still is located right where the Interstate 90, a.k.a. "The Pike," intersects with Washington Street.

Now, something else we need to know. Newton is an affluent and attractive community. The Cahners Building wasn't located in the *most* desirable part of the town in terms of residence, but it was the proverbial hop, skip, and a jump from there to the town center, which was quite charming. You could easily walk the distance, or jog it. Which he often did. The building had a little shower and locker room in the basement, and you could leave your stuff there, have a run during the lunch hour, and clean up afterwards. It was a very civilized place in those days.

Or, sometimes, when he wasn't in the mood for jogging, and he'd filed his stories for the week and so wasn't on deadline or anything, he would take an extended lunch (his boss was most understanding) and stroll down Centre Street to the little downtown area. There were cafes there, a fine bakery, and several shops whose wares he could not possibly afford, but which made for pleasant window-shopping.

The walks helped clear his head from the detritus of the job. He could sweep away all the cobwebs and trivia —the products with "new improved features" that no one really wanted, the interviews with narcissists in business suits and skirts, the glowing profiles of companies which might well be bankrupt in a year's time. Such is trade journalism on a bad day.

And, truth to be told, I...excuse me, I mean "he"... was having rather more bad days in journalism at that particular moment than had been the norm before in his life. It was a period of change and transition. Where, when he'd first gotten into the business, in the late '70s and very early 1980s, the computer press had been a delightful place, full of new magazines and with much hiring, now it was a bit grim. The great boom in desktop computing was over, and there were too many publications and not enough readers.

Thus it was that Cahners had begun the process of selling the name and assets of *Datamation*. Which meant that he and everyone else who worked there would soon be out of job. And, worse, given the realities of the market, he was not certain he would be able to find another full time job. Ergo, he had begun to consider the possibility of going freelance.

Which, oddly enough, brought up the question of ties.

5.

A note to complicate the fiction: he could not tie a tie.

He did not know why. Perhaps he was just not a spatial thinker. But whatever the reason, the four-in-hand, the Windsor, the half-Windsor, the Pratt...these were as mysterious to him as the dark side of the Moon. More so, since at least he'd seen a map of the Moon.

So, no. He could not tie a tie. When he tried, at best it looked sloppy. At worst, like he'd been recently but not quite competently hanged. As a result, when he absolutely had to have a tie around his neck, he affected a bolo and pretended it was an homage to his youth in the West.

However, just prior to this story's opening, there was a brief period when he did try to wear a tie on a regular basis.

It came about because of a wedding (and here is where we have the comedy). He had friends who were getting married South of Boston, on Cape Cod. It was complicated to get there from where he lived but he and his wife eventually worked it out. He would take Martha to work (she was a professor at Tufts) and then she would catch a ride south with other friends who were not going to the wedding but who did live in a town on the south side of the city.

He, meanwhile, would pick up their son from his school, gather all of the clothes and luggage, load up the car, and then drive across the state to meet her at the friends' house. They'd go from there to the Cape, spend the night, attend the wedding, and then drive back the following day.

Here, naturally, is where we have the first element of the comic, or even sit-comic. Here he plays the timeless role of the hapless TV husband and father, incompetent and bumbling. You may, if you like, join in with the laugh track or the compliant studio audience, giggling on cue. It is perfectly fine. He will not be offended. He cannot hear you.

Anyway, he knows that his assignment, the gathering of the clothes, is rather along the lines of do-and-die. If he doesn't get all of his wife's carefully prepared wedding outfit to her, and in good shape, he will never hear the end of it. So, he worked extra hard to make *certain* he had everything, and that none of it dragged or flopped to the driveway as loaded it.

After that, there was a rather nerve-wracking trip through the center of

Boston at rush hour on the Southeast Expressway. That was followed by a not much less anxiety-inducing attempt to find the friends' house and thread his way through of maze of road construction and seemingly identical suburban neighborhoods (recall, he is not a spatial thinker). Finally, though, he made it, and felt quite proud of himself for having made the trip successfully and not a forgotten a thing.

Except…

Except… as his wife pointed out (laugh track, chortle chortle, titter titter) as they sat in the friend's house and she regarded him with something less than complete sympathy…except for his own clothes. He had been so focused on getting her clothing successfully to Cape Cod that he had completely forgotten his own. His dress pants, dress shirt, sports coat, string tie…all were still back at the house. And he certainly wasn't going to drive back through the city to get them.

Fortunately, his problem was partially solved when they resumed their trip. Somewhere between the friends' house and Cape Cod they passed a shopping mall. He parked and he made a hurried assault on the various men's shops and men's wear departments. He soon had a new sports coat, slacks, and a dress shirt.

The one thing he couldn't find in a New England shopping center, of course, was a string tie. So, he bit the bullet and bought a cloth one. The next day at the hotel he dressed and fought with the tie. With much help from his wife and his son, he got the thing knotted in such a way that it almost looked as if he knew what he was doing.

The wedding itself went off with a hitch. And, at the reception, only one person…an older man…eyed the tie with some curiosity. It so happened that they ended up seated next to each another at one point during the evening. They made polite conversation. He watched while the man's eyes flicked time and time again to his throat. It must have been (he knew) torture for the other man to see the tie so ill-constructed. Like a crooked painting for a perfectionist.

The man wanted so badly, so *very* badly, to violate personal space, lean across and do the knot correctly.

6.

The tie was, thus, not a complete success. But it did start him wondering about ties. And about personal advertising.

When he returned from the trip, he reflected. If he did have to go freelance, might there not be things he could do to make the transition less difficult? Specifically, might not *ties* help him in his new venture? Not normal, staid, regular ties of the sort that everyone wears and no one really notices…but loud and colorful ones that stand out and stick in your mind.

He decided to perform a little experiment. He recalled that long, long ago, his parents had given him as a kind of joke-qua-birthday present a tie with pictures of Snoopy on it. He checked his closet. *Yes*. It was still there. Way in the back. On a hanger. He went online and discovered a webpage on Tying A Tie. He practiced at it for a couple of nights.

Then, he waited for an opportunity. It came the following week. He was scheduled to meet a vendor—that is, a company was sending its representatives to the magazine's offices to introduce some product or another in the hope that he would write about it—and he usually tried to get a little dressed up for such occasions. He wouldn't always wear a suit coat, you understand, but he'd usually try for a dress shirt and a bolo. However, he realized, the time had come for his little test. That morning, he extracted the Snoopys, tied them around his throat, and made his way to the Cahners Building.

At around 11 o'clock he went to his meeting. This time, the tie was a triumph. The two representatives of the company itself, stodgy executive types for whom gray was a flesh tone, seemed a bit stunned. He could see them trying not to stare. He enjoyed that. But the Public Relations woman, a person far more interesting than her clients, clearly loved his small affectation. "How wonderful!" she said and, and added, "He's so cute," by which she meant not him but Snoopy, that most excellent of dogs.

After that little victory, he began to feel a certain stirring of hope. Maybe…just maybe…he had the makings of an idea here. If he had to go freelance, maybe ties—wild and crazy ties—could be his *trademark*. Yes, yes! he thought. He would be that writer/editor of the Wild Ties. "Oh, you remember him," everyone would say. "He's that guy who always wears the crazy ties." Who knows? Maybe he'd have business cards made up with pictures of insane ties on the back. It would be a great gimmick. A sales tool *par excellence*.

But where the find the ties? That was the question.

7.

Next we must go forward, perhaps two weeks. It was a Friday, and, for once, he was in a relatively good mood. He had finished his work for the week and had turned in his feature ("Middleware Options For Distributed System Development") that morning. He was, thus, at leisure.

Further, it was a lovely fall day, not too hot, not too cold, so he decided to walk down to Newton and have a cup of coffee at a café. The scenery was good, the walk was energizing, and the coffee wasn't bad at all. He browsed the area a bit, looked into some of the shops, but went into none, and then decided he should be getting back to the office.

He started on his way…and then…he saw it.

The Charity Shop.

8.

The shop was a small place in a storefront along one of the side streets that led back from town-center to the Cahners building. It was quite out of the way, and he wondered how anyone ever even saw it. Yet, there it was. The sign identified it as being associated with one of the more well-meaning organizations in town.

He looked at the place. It had a big plate glass window out front, and written on the window in bright paint were the words, "Quality used women's *and* men's clothing." On the door, meanwhile, was a "Yes! We're open!" sign.

It seemed, however, to be empty and a little dark. He hesitated. Something didn't seem quite right, somehow. But then he asked myself, what on earth was he afraid of? Surely there was no one in there who'd bite him…though, that was a rather good idea for horror story. The werewolves of the second hand store.

Besides, if he wanted gaudy old ties, where better to look? Surely, if anyone had them, it would be a second hand store.

And that was *important*, wasn't it? Funky ties were going to be his calling card. It was going to be part of his career…the career that (he told himself) he was now going to manage like a pro. None of this drifting around on the winds of change, reacting as best he could to events. No! He was going to *take charge*.

So, he screwed his courage to the sticking place, and pushed open the door.

8.

It was dim and dusty. There were racks full of clothing here and there. At first he didn't see anyone, but then he realized that there were three women in the place. He supposed they were volunteer/clerks, not customers. In fact, there was little sign that anyone had bought anything in there for years.

He looked at the women. Two, he supposed, were in their middle sixties, and they stood in the back, straightening this and hanging that. The Third, an older woman, perhaps in her early eighties, was seated at a sort of desk or counter near the front of the shop. She was dressed to the nines, as they say. A severe, light beige suit. Her hair, very white, in a bob…

He smiled at them. The two in the back regarded him without apparent expression. Meanwhile, the old woman at the table studied him, also unsmiling, her eyes hard and glittering.

He greeted her. She nodded slightly.

He began looking around the shop. It was quite full...there was no end to the clothing...shirts, skirts, blouses, slacks...all stacked up in piles. It looked as though people had been bringing stuff here for years, but that none of it ever left again. The donations came, and here they stayed, patiently waiting...for what? For the end of the world maybe, when we shall all need new pants.

10.

He browsed a bit more. He poked at the piles...skirts that would have been in fashion twenty years ago, cotton shirts frayed at the elbows, a long and quite elegant (if enormous) gown that looked faintly as though it would have been at home at the inaugural ball of William Howard Taft...worn, perhaps, by the president himself, should he have had a taste for such things.

There were a few non-clothing items—bits of muddy-colored costume jewelry, a couple of paintings that seemed to have been done by very amateur hands, and some porcelain—meant for the dining table, mostly. There was a vast gravy boat, for instance, all done in a floral pattern and frills. Also, there was a kind of chicken thing, a covered serving platter or casserole dish, made in the shape of a hen. It was quite amazing, and if they hadn't priced it at fifty dollars he might well have bought it just for the wonder of the beast.

But there was no sign of ties.

He glanced at the three women. The younger two had returned to sorting and straightening. The older one, at her seat at the desk, continued to watch him unblinkingly.

He swallowed. He considered leaving. But, well, he was on a mission wasn't he? The shop was open to the public, was it not? And he was a member of the public. Besides, what could it hurt?

So, after a moment, he walked the desk and the old woman.

"I'm looking," he said to her, "for some funky old ties."

And then...

She annihilated him.

11.

It was the voice. It was the manner. It was the position of her head.

"That would require," she said, "that a) we carried men's clothing, and that b)..."

Well, actually, I've forgotten what "b" was. And what "c" was. In fact, there may also have been a "d" as well. But, I'm not certain.

In any case, it was a list of reasons why I...excuse me again, "he"...why he was an idiot to waste their time.

12.

Examined in retrospect, it was a rather an amazing performance, really. Without actually saying anything insulting, without rude gestures or raised middle fingers, she was devastating. She made him feel and look a fool. And it was done with far too obvious a delight, too broad a grin, to think that she did not enjoy the act tremendously. Indeed, one sensed that this ...the discomfiture of others...was her greatest pleasure in life, exceeding even Eros and gluttony.

Of course, too, as he realized when he considered the situation later, it was tactically and strategically brilliant. Because you are, obviously, helpless in such situations. How can you possibly respond? How can you defend yourself? This is An Old Woman. You mustn't be impolite to A Little Old Lady. You must indulge them. After all, She Is *Old*. She is Someone's Grandmother.

Society, therefore, gives her carte blanche. She is an old women. It's in the poem. She may wear purple. Spend the pension on brandy. Sit on the pavement and block the way. And it is fine. That is what we say she can do. She has license.

So...indeed, brilliant. Stunningly brilliant. And therefore, after a moment of fantastically strained silence while he considered his options, he did what we all do in such situations: Nothing. He said Thank You or I See or something else along those lines, and left the shop.

Does he hear as he leaves the sound of the three laughing at him? No. His hearing is not that acute. But it would make an excellent addition to the fiction. Let us, therefore, consider it possible.

13.

As he walked back to the office he analyzed the encounter as best he can. Eventually, he confined himself to three lines of speculation: 1) the nature of the shop itself and the social situation, 2) the woman herself and her motivations, and 3) the power of the social bully and his own weakness before it.

Let us take them in turn.

a. The Charity Shop

First, the shop. You run across these kinds of situations all the time, particularly when you start small non-profits, like the Charity Shop. You begin with good intentions. You staff with volunteers. Only, somehow, over the passing of years, the volunteers stop being interested in the business *per se*. The shop, the organization, becomes a kind of club where people go.

And such a place does good. Though it may not help the people for whom it was originally set up, it gives the volunteers a sense of belonging. A feeling of purpose. Even a sense of power.

The problem is that in such places, "customers" soon become intruders. And they are not welcome. They must be repelled. Driven forth. Removed.

As he had been.

b. The Old Woman

Second, the woman herself. He tries, as he walks, to make excuses for her. She is old. She may not be well. She confronts (as we all must confront at that age) her mortality. Or, a good Feminist interpretation of events (very trendy) her birth long predated the admission of women (or, at least, women a certain classes and races) into all aspects of society. Perhaps all her life she has been horribly frustrated by the fact that she could not rule in her own name… seek power and grandeur and achievement as her own person…be the woman on the cover of *Fortune* or *Forbes*. Such frustration, seething like acid just below her the surface of her flesh, could surely make any woman a vicious bitch at the very least.

And yet…

And yet he cannot quite believe that. There is something about her voice…that voice redolent with privilege and *very* Old Money…that makes him suspect she was nothing of the sort. More, her obvious comfort at his discomfort, the way she was clearly in command of the shop, her companions, and the situation, seems antithetical to the premise of her victimhood.

No. More likely (or at least so he senses) that she was one of those women who had no need to Feminism. She had been like (he suspected) one of those titanic dowagers of Victorian and European tradition, the grande *dames* who commanded estates and fortunes, and ordered about their sons and daughters and occasional husbands, and slept with the help if they felt like it.

So…no. Not frustration. More likely …less pleasantly…it was simply the way she normally behaved. So often her interactions had been not with equals but servants or other inferiors, that it never even occurred to her that she might have some obligation to be polite to someone beneath her station.

To someone, in other words, like him.

c. The Social Bully

Third, the problem of bullying. We...or most of us anyway...are governed by an unspoken set of rules and regulations. One is *not* rude to strangers if one can help it. One does *not* rebuke an old woman no matter how offensive she may be.

And, of course, the great power of the social bully is that he, or she, simply elects not to follow those dictums. The rest of us are helpless. We are paralyzed with shock when they behave so very badly. Then, we stumble and stutter, as we continue to play the game by the rules.

He wondered, later, what would have happened if he *hadn't* played by the rules. Suppose he'd responded exactly in the way she deserved? Suppose he'd leaned forward, placed on his hands on her desk, brought his snarling face close to hers and said, "Well, I'm terribly sorry. I was misled a) because it says, very clearly on your window, that you sell women's *and* men's clothing, and b) because I assumed that a civil question would be given a civil answer. And, oh, by the way, I assumed that c) a person of obvious culture and breeding would elect to behave according to the strictures of common courtesy...even with someone whom she assumed was inferior to her social station."

What would she have done? One wonders.

14.

He arrived at his office, returned to his desk, checked his email...

But he was not quite done with the Old Woman. As he sat there, at the desk, before the screen of PC, he wrestled with her memory. To his embarrassment, he discovered he took some (albeit small) pleasure in the thought that she is, after all, quite old, and would likely die soon. It was shameful thing, but he could not help it.

Indeed, he found himself constructing a rather elaborate fantasy about her, and about her passing. In his fantasy, it is not he who entered the Charity Shop that afternoon, but someone else. Some*thing* else.

The story goes like this: Once more the Old Woman sits in her seat, her throne, absolute monarch of her little domain. Someone enters. It is, perhaps, a man of indeterminate age. He is dirty and ragged. A street person. She regards him with distaste. How does he come to be there? she wonders. What does he want?

He appears before her, hat in hand, shyly. She notices that he has soiled himself at some time or another. His clothing reeks of dirt and oil and excrement. But he speaks politely, modestly. He asks where they might keep the men's pants.

She says, as she told me, that "a) we don't carry men's clothes, and b)..." etc.

The man pauses just for a moment. Then he seems somehow taller. He replies with my answer. "I was misled a) because it says, very clearly on your window, that you sell men's *and* women's clothing, and b) because I assumed that a civil question would be answered by a civil, rather than a mocking, answer…."

But then he does not continue speaking as I spoke. He comes to a very different item "c" than I proposed.

He says, "And of course you died five minutes ago."

She stares at him. "What?"

"As you sat there, your heart ceased to beat. Your breath ceased to come. You pitched face forward into your desk. Even now, your assistants huddle around your body in confusion and terror. They have phoned the police. They will be here in a moment. But it will be too late. There is no reviving you."

She opens her mouth to say something like "Don't be impertinent." But then she glances out the windows of the shop. She sees that Newton is no longer there. Instead, throngs of the newly dead make their way up the slopes of the Holy Mountain.

"Your path is there," says the angel, now revealed in all his shining glory. "You will arrive in time. But your journey will be longer than it might have been…"

15.

He was uncomfortable as he considered his fantasy. It was embarrassing. For one thing, it is badly written. Not one talks like that. Not even Death. Also, it is narcissistic. It transforms him into a divine being, an angel. Further, it implies that that the slightest affront to his dignity is a crime worthy of damnation. Or, at least, a few extra months in Purgatory.

Besides…

Well, suppose it was the other way around. Suppose it was not she who was to be tested, but he?

In this version of the story, he comes to her shop on that same day. And I …*he* makes his request for Funky Old Ties. And she gives her offensive response. And he is startled and embarrassed and walks away. Turning the other cheek as always.

But then, he reaches the door and pulls at the hand. It does not open. He struggles. It is locked. He looks behind him.

She is no longer the Old Woman. Instead, she is…Gabriel, perhaps, who is (or so I learn from Davidson's *A Dictionary Of Angels*) an angel of judgment.

She, as the angel, towers above him, all light and potency, and says, "If you had but shown a little courage, a little backbone, dared to disregard a rule, then all would be different. If you had...*for once*...told one of your oppressors exactly where they could stick it, then you would have discovered a new courage. A new forthrightness. A new relationship with the world.

"But, no...

"Once again, you do as you always do. You turn away. You avoid confrontation. You are soft and inoffensive. Spineless. Formless. You somehow convince yourself that cowardice is all for the best.

"So nothing will change.

"Return once more, therefore, to the world as you knew it.

"Or, if you prefer another name, to Limbo."

There is a flash. A rumble. And he finds himself once more upon the street. His life as eventless as it was before.

16.

Thinking thus, with himself (not her) now in the uncomfortable position of the damned, he decides to put the incident out of his mind. At 5:30, he leaves the office and drives home.

Now, move ahead in time and space. His magazine did, indeed, fold a few months later. But, he found another job, so he was spared going freelance for a while yet. He also abandoned the whole idea of the ties, funky or otherwise. Partly this is because he realized how ridiculous he looks in them. Partly, too, he remembered that he already has a trademark, if he wishes one—that is, his bolos, his string ties, which are every bit as memorable and striking as cloth ties could be.

And, also, partly...the Old Woman herself motivates him. Her interaction with him seemed somehow an ill omen.

And years pass.

17.

Now comes the hardest part. Now, I, the writer, and you the reader, must hold our breath and hope for the best while we attempt a startling transition. We must be, you and I, like trapeze artists. We are about to attempt a dangerous leap. You are one side of the swing. I, on the other. I will cast myself into space, turn a somersault, and reach for your outstretched hands. You must catch me. There is no net. If I fail to obtain sufficient momentum, I will fall. And the whole of this little effort will be for naught.

For, you see, it is here that I will to move from this little tale of a non-event, an unpleasant but meaningless encounter between two people, to something larger. To an abstraction. To social critique.

Ready? Here goes.

18.

In time, he moves out of the trade press entirely. He attempts to enter a couple of other professions. These include the Academy (he *almost* gets his Ph.D.), business, and even, as a volunteer for certain candidates, politics. In all these, he achieves various degrees of failure and success.

But, succeed or not, these forays educate him. As a journalist, he'd thought himself a hardened cynic. Seeing, however, these other trades from the inside (and particularly the university) he comes to understand how very naive he truly was, how much his cynicism was in fact a dreadful, nearly criminal innocence.

We will take first the academy (because that is where he went first after leaving the trade press). In his time there, he watches with a chilled fascination while certain members of the educated and the enlightened classes do and say the most horrific things…abuse and exploit their students, plagiarize papers, work actively and tirelessly to destroy colleagues for no reason other than purest spite, promote (more or less openly) various forms of totalitarianism, excuse massacre and terrorism… and then easily, oh-so-easily, justify their actions citing their attachment to certain, select groups. They are, you see, members of religious or ethnic minorities, or they endorse exotic political beliefs, or they were born of one gender or the other, or…well, a thousand other things. And this, they feel, gives them carte blanche to behave as they like, no matter how dreadful the consequences may be.

Do not misunderstand his position. Racism is real. Sexism is real. Homophobia is real. Class and poverty are real. Anti-Semitism is real…and, indeed, at least judging from the anonymous postings he has seen in way too many places on the web, is increasing. All these things exist and it is good to oppose them.

But what he has seen in the academy and among the intelligentsia is that the first people to claim martyrdom are distressingly often those who actually have very little reason to complain. They are…not always, but frequently…privileged men and women, who grew up with the very best of everything, went to excellent private schools (sometimes sent there in limousines), continued on to Smith and Columbia, and then, once they were adults, had the connections and contacts that everyone else lacks …so that, as if by magic, the jobs, the positions, the book reviews in leading publications, the editorships, the interviews on thoughtful chat shows just appeared.

At times, he has the urge to take certain of these people by the lapels and scream: "You are not who you say you are. You did not feel the whip.

You have never been in a concentration camp, or worked on a plantation, or lived on the mean streets, or been sold to the highest bidder at the Avret Bazaar. No matter how much your particular self-identified *group* may have suffered in the past, or suffers now someplace else, you, *yourself* have always been quite comfortable. You have never known real hunger. Or want. Or genuinely great pain. And there is something fantastically obscene about your use of someone else's anguish as an excuse for your own aggression."

But, of course, he does not say any of these things. It would be suicidal. It would end his career.

19.

And oh, by the way, it isn't just the academics, the intellectuals, and the political Left who are guilty of such behavior. No. Not at all.

During his brief foray as a volunteer in political action, he discovers that if the Left got an early start in the game of victimhood, the Right is catching up fast. Maybe already draws equal. Maybe has sprinted far ahead.

There is, for example, the Presidential candidate in the 2013 campaign who told wealthy donors that nearly half the American population would not take responsibility for their own lives—thus implying that they, the 47%, were without virtue and any discomforts they might have were their own bloody fault. As opposed to the donors, who, being rich, were clearly prudent and careful, the industrious ants to the lazy grasshopper, and rewarded accordingly by Heaven.

And then there was Australian billionaire who said that people should be willing to labor for $2 a day, and that those who critiqued the rich should stop complaining and simply work harder. The implication being, of course, was that she had earned her money by the sweat of her brow…she was worthy!…when, in fact, as a woman who had largely inherited her wealth, it was not clear how exactly how much she had ever perspired.

Also, there was the Silicon Valley venture capitalist who compared the wealthy to the Jews of Nazi Germany, and warned of a coming Kristallnacht for rich people. And there was the billionaire M&A real estate mogul who agreed with the Kristallnaht comment and added that the 1% simply worked harder than everyone else and so should be given their treasures without troubling complaints from the hoi polloi.

Then, too, somewhat earlier, after the financial meltdown of 2008, there were the Wall Street magnates who took vast sums in taxpayer money to prevent the wholesale collapse of the nation's financial infrastructure. The crisis had been created by those same people…yet, afterwards, they demanded multi-million dollar bonuses as "rewards" for their industry and imagination. After all, they said, they were important to the economy. Without them, they explained, God only knows what would happen to us.

Also, starting all the way back to the 1980s and the Reagan

Administration and enduring to the present day, there were the CEOs and corporate titans who impoverished entire populations, shipped industry and wages overseas, downsized and off-shored…and, through it all, complained that they were oppressed. They were job-creators (never mind the millions out of work) and the engines of creation (never mind the collapsing economy around them).

And on, and on, and *on*…an endless of litany of complaint, a chorus of the whining wealthy, the rich proclaiming their anguish …from the comfort of their yachts and mansions. They were *special*. They read their Ayn Rand and waved copies *Atlas Shrugged* and announced that it was upon them that the wellbeing of the world depended. How dare anyone fault them for their modest rewards—which they'd *earned*, after all, by their own hard work (don't look at the employees laboring in sweatshop conditions).

Again, do not get him wrong. He is no way anti-Capitalist. He waves not the red banner on the barricades. It is right to admire the innovator, the entrepreneur, the builder of businesses, the successful CEO who wrestles with the myriad problems of corporate survival in a complicated age…

But it is, surely, absurd for the rich to assume that their wealth came to them solely because of their own virtue. Or because some great Calvinist God decided they were the elect. No. Luck plays a role. As do connections. And inheritance. Much of America's elite is Old Money. Even the vaulted self-made man or woman often proves to be, if you do a little research, someone's heir. The number of "self-made" men and women who started out with a tidy little couple of millions tucked away in the bank is rather startling, as even the most superficial reading of biographies in the financial press will reveal.

Or…yes…sometimes, the entrepreneur doesn't receive *cash* from Mom and Dad. But money is not the only form of inheritance. He knows from his experience as a journalist how often the high tech creators of his day had received instead other things, often infinitely more important than mere capital. Like education. Like degrees from engineering or business schools. Like family connections in business. Like a childhood spent watching successful parents working in successful firms. Like, in short, the sort of knowledge that is not going to come easily to someone on the streets of Harlem or the back hills of rural Appalachia or the arid fields of an Indian reservation in New Mexico.

Ergo, for the wealthy to assume they belong to a uniquely moral group, to a community of superior virtue and superior genes, is laughable. For them to further assume that they are oppressed is grotesque. For them to conclude that the hunger and the poverty of others is merely a sign of moral deficiency on the part of the hungry and the poor is genuinely unforgivable.

20.

So it is that, two decades later, he remembers her. The Old Woman. The Old Woman who felt licensed by her privilege, her position, and, yes, her age, to be insulting to him...and to insult who knows how many others over the years.

He finds himself, one day, while considering her, making a stretch. He knows it *is* a stretch. Not really logical. He knows a reviewer or a critic would make very short work of his effort. But, even so, he forces the Old Woman into the role of Symbol.

He argues she was in no way unique. Indeed, she is the norm. She is at the very heart of public discourse in the West today. She is how we argue, and think, and debate what is moral and what is true.

What he fears is that we have come to a period in our history in which society has determined that select classes of people have the permission...or even obligation...to be, for lack of a better term, moralizing bullies. When he reads the magazines of the intellectuals, when he watches cable and searches the web, when he hears what passes for political speech in our capitols, he is struck by how often the subject being discussed is not what is good or bad, not what is efficient or in the national interest, not what is true and what is false...but rather which privileged group will have the right to be insufferable.

Or, to put it in language that is less emotionally charged, the debate is over which sub-groups within the National Political, Social, and Cultural Elite will take precedence...and with all the participants employing as their weapon in this struggle antithetical claims of unique virtue and unique oppression. Meaning: the battle is won by whichever member of the aristocracy can most successfully pretend to be the most common.

It is, in short, a war of shadows and lies...where unreality and fraud trump the obviously true...and the victor is the greatest of fantast of all.

21.

Indeed, he admits ruefully, and with no little shame, is he not himself guilty of the same sin? For how often has he used his status as a "creative individual" who is both blessed and cursed with "the artistic temperament," to justify some fairly awful behavior? Particularly towards his wife and family?

22.

It is distressing. It is unfortunate. It is a question: have we all become the Old Woman in Charity Shop?

And if so…is it healthy?

23.

We will abandon there him, there, my "he," the main character. We will leave him wondering about the social and cultural implications of a popular rhetoric based on …to put it bluntly…a kind of passive aggression.

But we are not quite finished, yet. We, too, have certain responsibilities. You must decide, for instance, if I (the writer) have been successful in my mid-course correction. Did I make the transition from story to un-story with any sort of grace? Did I (to return to my labored trapeze metaphor) launch into space, perform my death-defying feat, grasp your sweating palms with mine, and swing to safety? Or did I miss? Fall. Drop to the pavement. Where now the EMTs labor over my prostrate form.

Well, that is for you to decide. That is your task. I cannot be of assistance. I will leave you to it.

24.

But I, too, have work to do. I, too, must complete an assignment.

To wit, I (like my character) must worry.

As I end this fiction/non-fiction, as I walk away from my character, I must feel a chill knot in my gut. If I have been transgressive before, then now I pay the price. For I am required to ask the question that is the logical consequence of my indiscretion. Perhaps not ask of it of you. Perhaps only rhetorically. But I must inquire.

What happens…?

What happens to us, to our society, when finally someone or something appears …some genuine angel, or its antithesis…some agency human, organic, or mechanical…who cuts no slack? Accepts no excuses?

Strides unhesitatingly on great, sharp, metal feet toward the old woman blocking the pavement.

Does not slow. Does not step aside.

Does not care that she…or anyone … has the right to wear purple.

HELIOGABALOPOLIS

As everyone knows, shortly after the Singularity, with all its attendant confusions, trans- or post-humanity spread through the multiple matrices of space-time which proved (again as is obvious) not so much a continuum as a series of linked but discrete quantum realities. And, as shall be further recalled, among those pioneer post-humans, some possessed what might be called the fallen (cybernetic) angel's flaw, which is to say, the characteristic of creativity (so much the bane of transhumans and demigods), and for their efforts we must contemplate the fabulous works that so often typify the realities of transhumanic aesthetics.

The scholar points, for example, to such masterpieces as Trigon Three's "Ovulating Sun," with its disk of crystalline pseudo-planets, all mirroring and yet distorting (as is the role of children and similar demurragic creations) the beauty of their mother; and Mu Alpha's "Far Labyrinth," that region in which normal 3-space has been expanded by several additional dimensions, among them three spatial, two temporal, and the last (shall we say) wholly ambiguous and based (or so we believe) on some inexplicable violation of the Pauli Exclusion Principle—which is to say, possessed of a fury of ill-disciplined Fermions, each in perpetual if petulant disobedience of Fermi-Dirac statistics.

Equally acknowledged by the scholar are the artist collectives of the period. The scholar in particular is put in mind (or, if transhumanic, the minds) of the Seven Disciples, whose role as aesthetic demurrages is justly if (as some critics suggest) rather too violently celebrated. But, violent or pacific or incomprehensible, theirs is the work we most often consider as among the best of the early transhumanics, when the possibilities of the amplified human or constructed mind (today wholly blended) were as yet unexplored save by theorists of Neuroinformatics and Applied Semiotic Cybernetics. What is less known is that they, too, had their period of apprenticeship, when they were young, uncertain, and, unsure. They had, in short, their failures.

For example, let us consider the City of Heliogabalopolis.

As is well known, Heliogabalopolis was constructed along with its inhabitants by the Disciple Ashkelon, a.k.a., He Of Swans and Disciplines. Of Ashekelon himself, alas, we know little, and even that remains unilluminated by theoretical and interpretative apparatus. We must rely only on what he (assuming that he is a he) tells us in passing, plus the occasional newspaper account. Thus, most Ashelonologists posit that he or she or it had his or her or its origins at the very beginning of the Singularity, when machines were becoming first self-aware, and humans were expanding their own intelligence with bioprobes and neurolinks. And, so, we presume that sometime in the distant past, Ashkelon was either a network of rad-hardened military computers in concrete bunkers or, else, a cocktail waitress named Flo. Six of one.

But, to return the topic at hand, Ashekelon determined to construct a City wholly beautiful, noble in conception, and aesthetically compelling, yet, with a certain air of melancholy, as if its stone walls, mud huts, and marble palaces were themselves aware of the finitude of existence (oh ye mighty look upon my works). Thus, as Ashekelon conceived it, Heliogabalopolis (named for the long-dead emperor) was to be a city of purple and black, with overtones of white, and here and there a hint (like a splash of blood) of scarlet. It would be chill, both in climate and temperament, yet its history would be marked by those sudden and terrifying outbursts of violence, conflict, riot, mass lust, and quiet murder which are the inevitable companions of admirable restraint. Its people (built atom by atom, cell by cell in the nanofactoriums of Ashekelon) were to be dark-eyed, ebon-haired, lavender-skinned, and possessed of a taste for occasional illicit conjugation, as well as a tendency toward drama in politics, and as a people sensitive in the main but with a fatal attraction for Sartre's god of flies and death.

The City itself, meanwhile, with its towers, palaces, shadowed gardens, hovels, sports stadiums, race courses, squares, churches, pagodas, synagogues, mosques, and temples of secular speculation would be arranged in concentric circles, each in turn linked by roads, canals, moving sidewalks, funiculars, and sedan chairs. Further, it would be eternally in twilight, though whether of dawn or evening was left deliberately unclear. (It was positioned, you see, at the pole of a non-rotating but heavily terraformed world, eternal darkness on one horizon, eternal hint of sun on the other.)

And, at its center, in a white onyx basin, fed by channels, Martian canali, and the synthetic cataracts of an artificial Nile, would be a vast and circular pool of bitter water (dark, ice-flecked) that would, at its focus, vanish into a vortex maelstrom, a whirlpool, linking (perhaps, it is uncertain) to a subterranean river running not to the sea but the hearts of distant and unnamed mountains… and from there to oblivion and silence.

And, after a century, Ashekelon completed his City, and found it good, and was pleased, and switched it on.

Thus, as directed, the City lived. Princes demanded submission. Courtesans seduced the unwary. Assassins performed their invaluable civic function. Artists produced portraits of queer perspectives. Academicians waged their tedious wars over trivialities. Great families battled, and their children (whose love for one another was predictably denied) sought suicidal solace. It was all quite perfect and even a minor critical success.

But, gradually, Ashekelon grew unsatisfied with his creation. Was there not—he wondered—something banal in all of this? A thousand thousand cities before have had their princes, their courtesans, their assassins, their artists, their academicians, their great families and tragic lovers in the metro morgue. How was Heliogabalopolis different from those?

Alas, he concluded sadly, it was not. The City played out a script long ago written, long ago rehearsed to exhaustion, long before played to packed houses, and long before descended into cliché.

Very well. He determined, then, he would add something. He would arrange a Development, an action gratuite of shocking inexplicability, combining the sexual, the vehement, the mystical or at least the mysterious. Yes, he would engage in the supreme risk of creation—that of melodrama. Or, more precisely, archetype.

Ergo, Ashekelon manifested himself in his Fortress of Solicitude (constructed from prismatic fragments of coherent starlight hand-collected by diligent photovores who inhabit certain spaces beyond Sirius) and assembled there his many minions, assistants, cyber-cherubim, syntha-seraphim, automannequins, etc., and set to work upon a fabulous femme fatale of infinite cunning and boundless allure…i.e., a Medina-Medusa devouring female, Freudian, castrating, phallic mother, She Who Must Be Obeyed, equally the horror (albeit for different reasons) of misogynists and feminists. She was completed in seven days. (On the eighth, he rested.)

And when finished, even his harshest critics would confess that she was magnificent. Skin dark to the point of purple. Hair cropped and dark to the point of jet. Eyes dark to the point of obsidian. A face lovely to behold, yet chill and charged with a vast potential for erotic cruelty. Firm breasts. Flaring hips. Nude save for black latex hip boots (high heeled, naturally) and a black leather belt with holsters for twin hollow needle stiletti each charged (of course!) with their requisite dosage of explosively driven sodium cyanide. Less often, though frequently at state functions and fancy dress dinners, she would carry as well a riding crop and/or a sjambok whip of the sort constructed of rhino penis.

Ashekelon, noting and approving the illumination of madness in her eyes, introduced her, "like Lenin or a bacterium," into Heliogabalopolis as a foreign princess rumored to be, in fact, the illegitimate daughter of the Old Grand Duke, the one who disappeared while hunting hydra and heraldic griffin on Planetary Night Side. She gained lovers, followers, political supporters. Women and intellectuals cheered her as the destroyer of outmoded stereotypes. Generals approved the toughness of her pronouncements and editorials regarding the need for air strikes and commando raids on the libraries of the seditious. Merchants thought well of her quotations from Ayn Rand. Moreover, she appeared on all the late night talk shows and radio demagogues declared her fit for highest office.

The coup was well planned. The Palace Guard rose in rebellion. The streltsy, cuirassiers, demi-lancers, harquebusiers, and paratroopers were all on her side. Students left their universities and joined with the workers in the streets. Retailers shuttered their shops and the Malls refused to open. Barricades appeared and ineffectual academics were seen in cafés waving new written manifestos.

Thus it was that history was formed and spectacle provided. The audience gathered for the final act (so carefully prepared). The femme fatale, now Queen, stands spread-legged, hands on her hips, still nude, still in the black boots, but up to her calves in the cold water of the Central Pool with its Vortex. She delights, laughs, to the cheers of the assembled multitudes on the banks as the six children of the former royal family are drowned by soldiers and one by one vanish into the inky depths. The babies make bubbles as they go.

But, then, just as the last is gone, there is An Unexpected Development—something unplanned, something unforeseen, something not within the script so tenderly edited for continuity by Ashekelon.

The Queen stiffens. She gasps. She feels a pain in her Achilles heel. She reaches into the water and pulls from beneath its turbulent surface a marine creature…something like a lamprey, something like a squid, about the size of a trout, covered with hard toxic spines like those of a Lion Fish or a Stone Fish or certain carnivorous gastropods listed in obscure texts. Ashekelon has not designed it. Ashekelon has not permitted it. Ashekelon does not know from whence it came. Yet, inexplicably, it has pieced the Queen's boot. It has cut to the bone. Already, the Queen feels the venom in her blood. The coldness is horrific. With a scream of fury rather than fear, she pitches forward into the waters, then vanishes into the maelstrom, joining the princely kindertoten in their special darkness.

Ashekelon, who is watching all from hyperspace, sees developments and is aghast. How has this occurred? Yet, it is only the beginning of his reverses. The assembled multitudes, the citizens of the city, gaze on the scene and then, silently, return to homes and offices. Over the days that follow, they take up their tasks and former lives. Yet, there is a hopelessness in them, a queer misery. They lack their customary fevered vigor. The City knows, for the first time in its existence, an airless, sad, and meditative lethargy.

In time, the People cease to breed. Some die by their own hands. Others, most, simply take to their beds, or blindly wander empty streets, and perish from a lethal despondency. Heliogabalopolis The Mighty is no more. Its glass towers and concrete domes crumble. Strangling vines obscure its features. The Great Cathedral becomes the abode of serpents and scorpions. The crystal pool silts into a mire.

Ashekelon, for a time, is bewildered. But, then, in consultation with his colleagues of the Seven Disciples, he realizes his error. "Images," they explain, "once created, have a logic of their own." The City must wrestle with its underlying artistic banality. The Queen must be created to challenge the resulting predictability. The Princely Children must die to provide the obligatory pathos. Poison must appear for the dramatic conclusion. The City must perish to atone.

Thus it was that…chastened, wiser… Ashekelon and the Seven turned to other things—indeed, some of the greatest of their Masterworks date from this period. Critics are, therefore, grateful to the City and its errors. Without it and them, would Ashekelon have yet created such tours de force as The Sabine Bacterium? The Semotic Storm? The Bitterwood Envisionment? Assuredly not.

Yet, alas! The critic and historian must record one final failure for Ashekelon. It must be mentioned that as a last, redemptive erasure of Heliogabalopolis, its Creator decreed Rain. Not of water, but of glass…which erupted hot and molten from uncharted volcanoes on the inner moon. In the twinkling of an eye and a moment of flame, Heliogabalopolis was made naught, replaced for all eternity by the Mountains of Transparency.

But, even then the City's mischief was not complete. Visitors to that world report that one may stand upon the Mounts and, on occasion, see a flickering of lights, a hint of shadow in their depths. Press your face downward to the glass (as if in homage), and, just as the rejected portrait bleeds through the obscuring gesso, so, too, appear before you the images of princes, courtesans, assassins, artists, academicians, tragic lovers, Criminal Queen and tender Kindertoten.

Ergo, the lesson of Heliogabalopolis, learned well by the Seven and all who follow them: to wit, Beware Creations Too Fondly Imagined. For they have vigor. Which is to say they are possessed of the deadliest foes of perfection…

Volition, motion, and memory.

Note: this story originally appeared in in Issue Three of the 5923 Quarterly

March 2011, 5923quarterly.net/issue3/heliogabalopolis.html

FLASHES

Ghost. Dog. Virgin.

When I was actually rather old for it, in fact, in my next to last semester in graduate school, a young woman who I was attempting to seduce asked me if I were a virgin. Surprised in the car as I drove her back from our class in common, I did not answer, which silence she (of course!) interpreted correctly and, then, she explained without embarrassment that she had requested the ride specifically that she might pop the intolerable question when my answer or lack thereof would not be overheard as I stammered and flushed. We arrived at her destination and she left without further comment, though instead possessing a smile, discrete and chaste, at my expense.

Most distasteful for me, obviously. Yet, years later, even when I had graduated on to the more normal condition of men in my society, I began to wonder if I might owe something to my inexperience, to the ancient and seemingly invincible naivety which kept me, in my way, a pimpled adolescent well into my twenties (and perhaps beyond). As my career progressed I found that it, and I, were greatly driven by my shame...by, that is, the shadow of that hard dying virginity. Its memory pursued me. Somewhere I actually began an essay in which I believe I compared it to "the ghost of a dog," invisible normally, but seen while waiting for a bus in a light rain at Haymarket station, the mist forming the outline of the beast as it followed me into the yellow pool of light provided by the street lamp.

I never, however, completed the essay, preferring instead to keep so powerful an image on the shelf, as it were, awaiting another piece, in which it might stand as a symbol of something that embarrassed me less, perhaps my own mortality and death, and when I do get around to using it, I shall (I think) employ it as an ending, an epilog, in which I see the crystal skull floating, eyeless and fanged, just inches above my own face, as I recline in a troubled sleep in the back bedroom of that terrible little apartment we had in Lynn.

This piece originally appeared in 751 Magazine, Dec 2009. http://751contents2.wordpress.com/issue-2/tucker/

Macbeth, Medea

My being born to them (with my set of what it is now polite to call Special Needs) was like, I suppose, coming already circumcised from the womb to a family of anti-Semites, and, anyway, later, I wondered how it happened at all. I suppose it was some trick, shall we say, of vanity, and thus they did not give me up for it would have extracted, as it were, the nails from the palms too soon. So, they clenched their fists protectively, the blood seeping between their knuckles, and he spent ever longer hours at the office, while her writings turned increasingly to Macbeth and the exit scene of Medea at her vengeance, dwelling in particular on the dragons supposed to have drawn her chariot to heaven.

This piece originally appeared in A-Minor Magazine, aminormagazine.wordpress.com/, June 6, 2011

Found Photo

Shortly after her death—she refused to give up cigarettes, even as she was on oxygen—you are going through her papers and you discover that she had only one photo of you. You almost over-looked it entirely (it was mixed in with her clippings, newspaper accounts, reviews of her second book) and it fell into your hands by accident. It showed, however, you at about age four, maybe three. In any case, you are very young and you are seated at the kitchen table in a booster seat. You are weeping. Your hands cover your eyes and your mouth is open. It must date from just about the period of their second, and in the end, final separation. She told you, in fact, that he had died, and later, when you discovered otherwise and sought him out at sixteen, your going to him was an act of real courage, rather like visiting the dead. But, how strange, you think, as you throw the photo away, that she had no pictures of you laughing, even though you distinctly remember being able to do so. But, no, only this. Your tears as bright and savage as molten glass.

This piece originally appeared in Shoots and Vines, Issue 4, Oct 2009, shootsandvines.com.

To the Tenured Professor on the Occasion of Her Complete Victory

We all have our sins, so, I suppose, I possess the possibility of damnation. I suppose, too, that my particular offense will be that of wrath or pride. Still, at least I know I have a place. Pearly gates may bolt and bar but those of Morningstar are wide and welcoming. Indeed, I may be proud. Does not Sartre say we specify our own secret or stated hells? And so unique chastisements… torments tailor-made…have surely been prepared for me. Personalized. To fill the endless, empty hours of all eternity. To spare me from infinite tedium. I will be tenderly cherished thus, with fire and tongs, by fallen angels and risen demons.

But for you, my dear professor, I cannot say the same. For you, I fear, awaits the fate of Dante's Vestibule, the place of those who select neither virtue nor transgression. I knew you first as friend. Then, others, more forceful than yourself (though they did not possess more power), commanded. And you, because you bend to the wind and the will of those who seem the strongest, you obeyed. You became therefore the villain of the piece. Though, I suppose (my last supposition for the day) that you most resemble not the monster but the jellyfish. Spineless, boneless, washed ashore and dying hidden, half-buried in the sand. Yet, your toxicity? Undiminished. And thus the running child with eyes only for the sea has no warning. Not until the sting. The pain. The searing of the flesh.

Salt

I saw you that morning at the moment of your triumph and I watched you with much curiosity, wondering why you had elected to be insulting when it gained you nothing. You could have simply sent a two line email and that would have done the trick. I'd have been gone. Yet, that wasn't good enough and I could not fathom why.

But, then, then, I began to understand. You are the Master of the World. Or, absolute master of your own world. That tiny world you have so carefully constructed. There, in the department that you head. There, with your tenure (say, why wouldn't they give it to you at Harvard?) and your teaching and your being "outstanding in your field" (say, why is it that you no longer edit that significant journal that used to give you such potency? That made you so feared?) Thus, your oh-so-civil cruelty. For no other reason save the bully's. Because you could get away with it.

So…emperor. There in your gelatinous magnificence. In your shadows. Your office. Your mildew and decay.

I await with real anticipation the coming of some titan…some giant boy, full of life, full of light, full of the sun. Who will in time (it is inevitable), discover you there, in the leaves, the rotting leaves in great wet piles just before the first snow. Who will find you, pull you out of your little kingdom, pull you squirming into the light, regard you with wonder, and with…and with…

A handful of salt.

Onychophora

When I was young my enemies and sometimes my friends (tenuous distinction) would compare me not to a summer's day but those small, strange animals, colorless, pale and huge-eyed (or not eyed at all) who dwell in caves, in that alternative world that knows not sunshine nor autumn rain. And I suppose, when I examine photos from my youth, there is admittedly a certain similarity. As I aged I lost the physical characteristics, though, not the comparison, and perhaps sensing the past by some skill of personal analysis, they ...the inescapable They of office and campus... inevitably discovered it, that sensitivity, and applied it, though now in whispers. Ghostly. Half-perceived at the proverbial water-cooler. The conversation not meant (was it?) to be overheard. Such is maturity. Such is professionalism.

But then, ah, but then, you. You became visible. You manifested yourself like that moment when the moonshadow departs and the burnished, the burning disk is again revealed. Gold. Copper. Helios. You appeared. And to their horror, by some magnificent transgression of the probable, my troglodyte love, "vaster than empires" etc., appealed to you. Somehow, unaccountably, inexplicably, enigmatically, I won you.

As I say, they were aghast. It was as if the cavefish, the blind salamander, the velvet Onychophora ... it was as if these, by some cunning enchantment, some trick of quantum theory, emerged quaking and fearful into the light, stood swaying for a moment, uncertain, in the torrent of the sun, yet found their footing, set forth...and behold, the luminosity did not burn but rather welcomed. Thus they begin their journey into the alien light. The exquisite exploration. The quest of the hero, who, after many trials, comes at last to the temple of the Sun where is found the Sleeping Queen.

Just so, you lead me into radiance. Just so, They, the others, they stand, blinking, half-blind, afraid, wondering at the meaning of it all. The meaning of the Day. The Morning. The emergence from Shadow.

Beach at the end of the universe

To describe my feelings for you, well, I suppose by indirection I might attempt it. And say that sometimes, now and then, I deal in magic. Not the real sort. Not the proper sort. Not the slight-of-hand, rabbit-out-of-the-hat, nothing-up-the-sleeve sort. That sort is pure and right. And honorable.

No. My dealings are in the place where fantasy and physics have their, well, illicit union (image: the hotel room, the rumbled bed, the smoldering, cancerous cigarette, Quantum and Conan. I mean the barbarian). I traffic, that is, in the Singularity. The center of— oh the fabulous melodrama of it, vaster than empires—the center of the universe. Where creation ends and begins and restarts with a sputter and a cough. God's great fuel injection engine. And the inhabitants? Of course, transhumantic: photovores and demigods, automated angels, cyborgs, postmen (not the kind with the letters, but rather post tense), and, oh, You Shall Be As Gods. And the frightening thing, of course, is that, when all is said and done, it will be true. Truer than anything I have written otherwise. Every word of it. All prophetic. The paradise of posthumanism.

Yet, I am not impatient. I do not long for the coming of these visions. I have no urge to enter the Electronic Eden. Because, you see, I have tasted better already.

I remember. That day at the beach. At the late summer, almost autumn beach when it was too cold for swimming and anyway we did not have the clothing for it. And I was in that ridiculous suit and tie after the job interview. But, you, dear, (dear heaven) you were in that dress that flowed like water, like wind, to your ankles and we walked, you, (my God!) in your sweetness and your magic. Your belly round as the sun with the baby we called already The Little Bear (how big he is now) and you had on those huge dark glasses and your sandals were in your hand, the hand that was not holding mine, because you wanted to feel the sand and sea.

And that, of course, is the truly singular. The genuine re creation. The actual center. And the angel? The angels. You and he. In your mirror you perceive them. You, who are eternal, young, strong, wise, beautiful, tender. And on that beach I will be with you forever. There, where the past, the present, the sun, the ocean, where all opposites attract and reconcile.

Thus, through you, I have obtained my material salvation. You are my true and genuine Jerusalem. Shining. Incorruptible. Treasure.

Pearl of infinite price.

Bath

You came to the old house. I did not hear you enter. You were silent. I go there only in autumn. Only in passing. The bath is antique, black with clawed feet, a fabulous, Victorian monster. There are red copper pipes. There is a shower. I emerge from the needle spray. Draw the curtain. You are there.

I had thought you were in the city. I thought you would not come. I thought you had other plans. You have never come before. But now. You are here. In the blue Chinese robe we bought in San Francisco that spring we visited and you feared to drive the coast road.

It falls from your body.

Such is magic. Such is wonder.

on an island otherwise invisible

For me, you are like, oh, an old Chinese fairy tale, the kind in which the young student is crossing the lake and the boat sinks and he finds himself on an island otherwise invisible and he meets you as you come down the path, you are the child of the rain, your crown is red coral, your gown is yellow silk, your elaborate wings are bronze inlaid with gold, your smile incomprehensible, your lips on his, your nipples hard and sweet under his tongue, your orgasm intricate, violent, complicated.

And, of course, years afterwards, a sister will claim to have seen him in dreams, seen him married to the daughter of a dragon and living in great splendor and the crystal palace requisite in such stories. But, wisely, the student's friends will discount the testimony of she who loved him as a child, will instead assume him drowned, or devoured by a kraken, though they will do so with a certain uneasiness, each knowing in secret that they would rather have him dead than quite so enviable.

This piece originally appeared in Chapter Seven of The Anemone Sidecar
ravennapress.com/anemonesidecar

Arctic

Later that day I had, well, call it a vision. I envisioned her as, well, as she would be, would have been, if I were her lover. I envisioned, say, her outside on a day with snow. The flakes on her face. Eyelashes. I envisioned myself, not as myself, of course, but as the person I would have had to have been for her to see me.

And the vision left me with such satisfaction in its sadness, so intense, so self-pitying (yes, without apology), that I derived from it something close to the passion which is otherwise denied me.

And, thus, I was able to enter work the next morning, curiously at ease, familiar with her, and yet distant, as though I had been already transported to some remote place in the north, a place of abandoned derricks and rigs, and I stood upon the ice, unconcerned, and watched as already the long white fingers of winter and cold and night came up the valley to where I stood

without shelter.

without desiring it

bats

Her dying was like, well, it was as if our two bedroom apartment (already crowded with you, me, the baby) had been suddenly inhabited by, to use the scientific term, an "emergence" of bats, hordes and hordes of them, a swirling, numberless intensity, tiny and furred, like, oh, a childhood memory of a visit to Carlsbad, and they would surface to feed at dusk, an infinity of leather drumhead wings, but captive, in the two rooms plus half bath and kitchenette, swirling, densest most in the hallway that led to her bedroom, and we would move through them into the living room or the bath with our hands thrown up over faces to protect our eyes, sometimes pause to beat at the air, feel the sudden bite to the bone, the flicker, the flutter, the trickle of blood, the sound of her breathing.

Confessing the Alternative

it is a curious thing confessing

      fidelity, to attempt, however uneasy, exactly why it was that i declined that afternoon, when she called up all of sudden and said would i join her for lunch? a picnic, perhaps, and i met her, there, at the park where the small pool from the Charles comes up behind the Science Museum. we sat, crossed legged, side by side on the grass. i critiqued her resume. we ate sandwiches.

      our legs touched. she leaned to me. we were head to head as peered at the page. and, strangely, faking an innocence i do not possess, i did not do as i might have.

and, it was difficult for me to say why

A memory of drowned sailors

Later, I think, they realized their marriage was a complete sham, in that, at least, they loved one another no more than one might the furnishings of an inexpensive room, that is, not so much adored as endured, and if the plastic dining table, the stain-proof sofa, and the coin operated magic fingers should, somehow, vanish bit by bit, as this or that guest walked out with the ashtrays or the towels, it really didn't matter much, because it all came out on the tax returns.

Yet, in the end, they were content because they knew also they possessed a bond more tight, enduring, and lasting than love, or us, the children, or the shared investments that not even the accountants and real estate lawyers could pry apart. Rather, they clung, as might eighteenth century shipwreck victims, lashing themselves together on either side of a single bit of flotsam (or is it jetsam?), a barrel, perhaps, or an overturned table.

And though it all, through the disasters of the 60s and God! the twenty years after that, they clung, eyes closed, teeth clinched, green sea foam on their hair and their lips, giving them at times an alien beauty, like that of the drowned dead, scaled flesh and deep blue shadows, knowing, clinging tightly in the knowledge that the alternative was worse, sleeplessness, insomnia alone in beds too big for them.

Paradise 1

she wore, in those days, soft baggy pants that ballooned out around her
legs but came close and tight around her buttocks. it was a style of the
period and I confessed, once, that in the guise she reminded me
of the Eden character in the 60s sitcom about the domestic
jinn, and i named her such. saying that her lover (which
i was not) saying that her lover should
name her ...taking Adam's power of naming... should name her
Paradise. should name her Eden or Earthly Paradise, both for the pleasure
he would find within her, but also for the wilderness of it, that
she was like, say, some pirate's vision of Belize, a wild lush green
tangle of flowers, and vines, and small rivers inhabited
by jewel finned fish of scarlet and indigo

entropy

the obscure eros was like oh, like being one of those cosmologists who do not accept the concept of the closed universe, in which ultimately everything collapses upon itself and Big Bangs out again in a regular rhythm of celestial immortality (the beating, if you will, of the eternal heart of Shiva), and instead, mounted on an algorithm, you take the road of entropy beyond its logical conclusions, deep in fact into the dark itself, on the other side of the decay of supposedly elemental particles, riding the math until the model collapses (the algorithms twitching compulsively) below you, you struggle to your feet, go on in the dark, touching the walls with your hands because you can see nothing, until, pausing, you hear something in the distance, a movement on the road ahead, and then, improbably, it stands dark and sinister as id in front of you, glowing somewhere just outside the visible spectrum, in the infra-red probably, and you recognize, suddenly, with the twist in the gut, the mirrored face it wears upon its own.

Transgression 7

that day we drove out to the ice cream place, and, while parked near the lake, she, well, responded to my question by leaning over in her seat and sinking face downward into, well, not to put too fine a point on it, my pants. and, afterwards, in a gesture of almost fantastic obscenity, licked her lips. and for me it was, well, an odd confrontation. as if she weren't there at all, really, in spite of the pink flash of the tongue, then the variant of the classic mona lisa smile. as if, instead, i stared into the rear view mirror angled downward to see myself and saw ... well, something ... like, I suppose, like being Uncle Walt's wicked queen, peering into the smoky glass, seeing there not the gentleman expected, but snow and the spirit, the latter already withered and corrupt, as though the tale were told by a Wilder sort of Grimm.

invisible letters

later, of course, i would wonder would you have said the things you did in the way you said them, had you known that he came that day with a pocket full of love letters, which, that is, he'd written at the office on company time when he should have been using the word processor to do billings. But, of course, there was no way for you to know that. And, besides you'd been home all day with her. So, you were waiting in ambush by the time he hit the door, prowling, sniffing the ground, tracking the fight like a ferret after a rat, going for his eyes, well, metaphorically, anyway, the minute he was past the welcome mat. And, all through it, your mother sat on the couch, chainsmoked her godamn black russians, and read in one hand (she holds it the same way when she pisses) a paperback mystery noted mostly for its mutilated nudes.

couple

I knew them both some years ago. He, the husband, trembled on the edge of adultery like a butterfly in a high wind. She, meanwhile, she lived so completely up to the cliché, the stereotype of the suburban upper middle class matron, involved with her causes and good deeds, the defense of rain forests and colorful peoples in distant locations, that in a sense she had transcended them, become somehow her own parody, and knew something akin to the divine in this terrible perfection.

Symbolic processor

One night, some weeks after the final interview, when you know your story was already published (and indeed already obsolete in light of the additional resignations) you seem somehow returned to that immense, bunker-like office building just on the edge of AI-alley, across the way from MIT, but, this time, it is after, not before, the second set of lay-offs, and there is a maze-like quality to everything. You are left for days in the lobby, the guards and the receptionists eye you curiously, when suddenly seven flacks appear from nowhere and hustle you into a elevator. They speak in chorus and in unknown tongues and lay hands on you and vanish and next you know you're in a wilderness of rooms without windows. Finally, behind a Xerox machine, you come to a green metal door. It slides open soundlessly to reveal the office of the Great Man. You find him face down on the desk, blank purchase orders before him blotting up the seepage. You notice that the screen of his monitor and his keyboard have been stained, as if he'd attempted some final communication. You lean forward to read it. The screen swarms with complex diagrams. Arrows. Boxes. Tasks. Data flows. It flickers, fades, goes finally to an empty amber-green.

San Diego

you are -- forgive me -- wasted in Boston. You are rather the sort of person who should be someplace, well, not exactly tropical, but close to it, anyway. San Diego, perhaps. Or Belize. But, anyway, the sort of place where the honey colored light might slant down on you, through the ancient, almost prehistoric palms, (ferns, actually, and there should be giant dragon flies among them, huge and delicate and beautiful as chinese kites) and you float in water which is just the temperature of blood, and then you rise, one deliberate step at a time, up the concrete stairs, to the deck, and I meet you, wrap you with the great pink hotel towel, you are nude, I caress you, I pull the rough soft cloth across your back, smooth it over your nipples

merciful love

Toward the end of the second year at his first real job, he became dangerously infatuated with a young woman in the office, the assistant of the national director, who, it seemed to him, had expressed a certain interest in him. Later, he would discover that she was, in fact, a real-life femme fatale, that semi-mythical creature who has been driven to near extinction by literary critics, and so has had to abandon fiction entirely, taking up residence instead in her ancient and impregnable fortress, reality.

Anyway, he learned later that she had a certain thing for married men. "It got quite messy, last time," a friend of hers would tell him. But he, fortunate soul, was spared that because at the time he was not married. And, besides, after an initial burst of flirting, she began to avoid him. And, not long after, she took a higher paying job (and a lover) in another city.

At the time, he took his failure with her as further evidence of his own romantic inferiority, that certain lack of an essential animal something that kept him single and dateless long after other men had ascended once or twice into marriage and/or divorce. But, as he learned more about her, he began to realize that, no, she had let him go. He realized that he had managed (surprisingly) to touch whatever it was that approached her affections, and that as she had contemplated him as he hung there, spinning and twitching at the end of the thread, she was moved, and, atypically, allowed him to drop before the final bite.

Thus his eternal triumph. He, as so few had before or since, had inspired in her a genuine passion...expressed, demonstrated, by his sudden fall to earth, the impact, the blood, the confusion, the closest thing to a caress that anyone living or dead would receive from her.

Bathysphere

Oh, my dearest, dearest, most cherished enemy, you who did me the greatest damage for the least reason, who would have brought about my utter destruction had it been in your fortunately (for me) limited power, I fear for you. I have seen the hidden parts of you. In my banishment I have discovered much. And I should have guessed it before. How often, that is, I saw you in passing, your young woman's face somehow ancient, on verge of tears, "no loathing like self-loathing" you told me once, and I think you meant it.

And then you sought my obliteration because I was, you said, unprofessional. But come, let us be honest. We both know the real source of your detestation. It was because once, in a small room, before a small crowd, for just an instant…I…I took the spotlight from you. And had I known at all…had I known in the least…had I known remotely…how desperately you needed that feeble illumination to compensate for the all-consuming darkness, I never would have done it. Never would have earned your deathless, endless, infinite enmity. Would have let you be the sole and solitary radiance. Let you be like those hideous fishes, great jawed and huge-eyed, that glow greenly and faintly at great ocean depths, observed only by crab or kraken. Or by some passing explorer, some strange, unwelcome visitor (as I was strange and unwelcome) in bathysphere or diving gear.

So you arranged my exit. Or, more precisely, tipped me into hell. And I confess. I confess to hating you for a time. I confess (perhaps) to hating you still. But, on reflection, not as much as I might. Your misery, your tragedy, defangs me. For here is the reality I have discovered. My brimstone revelation. What I have learned in secret, shadowed places. My hell is more comfortable than yours. And I did not labor, as you have labored, to construct it. With sweating brow. And bleeding fingers.

pool

shortly after sending you the letter, and wondering what you would answer, I was waiting for a friend at the Ground Round down on the corner -- he never showed -- and had a vision of you reclining on the the red pillow, on the bed, and I would place a drop of oil at the base of your throat, just under the Eve's Apple, watch it slowly descend, pass between your breasts, come to rest, finally, as a kind of motionless, vibrating pool in the rim of your navel, rising and falling in a sort of tidal effect with each breath, then disturbed most by the finger I draw across the oval of your belly

Princess

to console you on that day of, well, not exactly personal tragedy,
but

misfortunate, when you wore a costume of spring colors in the
strangely

delayed, warm winter day, the pink suit coat, the white tights, the
small

leather slippers, very arabian nights and victorian explorers there
on shore

of the unknown African sea, source of the nile, white mountain, I
told you that on the day I created my own nation in a warm
climate (sea breeze, salt water image of of prenatal, primal
ocean, I like lung catfish walking, lobe finned on white beaches) I
would grant you instant citizenship, more, decree feasting, proclaim
you princess, crown you with silver, adorn you with baltic
amber, name you protector of Atlantis, defender
of Ophar and Oz

promethean

       meeting on what we hoped was the last day of the warm weather, we found ourselves driven from the picnic by the cold. So, abandoning the hill side, the grass, the old splay-legged cat that begged for bits of the turkey, we fled, pursued, in fact, by, if you will, the feeble demons of an early winter (bloodless off spring of the frost giants, now extinct) following us to the car, pressing their immaterial white fingers against the windshield. And, in the end, we were undisturbed, anyway, for, like twining greenhouse ivy, we possessed the promethean secret of illicit heat.

SOMETHING LIKE POETRY

Angel and Alice

I envision you as Alice
in her final incarnation after the
looking glass, after Wonder-
land, that is to say, as
the Angel Uriel
seen passing,
at the end of time,

envision
you as seen in flight,
across a sky in
storm, just at sun-
set

envision you,
as you speed from
the dark horizon to the lighter,
counter clock-
wise, anti-
matter time,
from the night to afternoon,
as she hunts the blood-
red sun,

envision you
wings apple-
green, jadeite,
emerald butterfly,
wings as intricate and delicate as
a Chinese robe, I

envision you
flight
passing

to the West, and I,
the Great White Rabbit,
man-
slaughter hare of
Hieronymus Bosch
shamble like a bear,

there

At the end of all things

Amherst

years later,
I would go to a small bed and
breakfast, outside of Amherst, I
would walk up the road there,
through the fields of strawberries,
accompanied by a great dog that
attached itself to me, it
would rest its head against me, I
thought of you, in passing, how,

in fantasy, of course, you are there

To explain

To explain the adult, one must
mention history, so,
my adolescence would
make bad fiction, it contained no tension
in the lines
Only,
a kind of Syriac silence,
or maybe Coptic,
but anyway, of
rooms shaded from the light of a sun
too much the desert
god, and books, like a Borges library,
history, fiction, science, so that the
past was open to me,
the future closed, and I lived
as the apex of a crystal pyramid, suspended
over limitless space, above me
the world contracted,
a primal singularity, Black
Hole, the official term, consuming
possibility, scarlet with Hawking's
after glow

I am without promise

Apology

It was, of course, the wounding

of the innocence that hurt the most, a
sort of bruise of the brain, a purple blood
red shadow on
the relationship, injured
with an excess of affection, like,
oh, say,

the touch of a boxer, on
the end of a long life's punch
drunk,

clumsy, unpracticed with tenderness,
or,

it was like an ill-timed bout of
sickness, on the part of someone
weary

from one too many mid-night dashes
to someplace between
the hospital and the cemetery, and
not even the disease is his possession,

and who, in
the midst of sleep,
sometimes feels the dusting
of a Boston winter,
placing gently,
over his eyes,
the silver pennies
of that final ice

Bath

to astound me
on that morning, in the
old house, I go there
only in autumn, the shower-bath is
an antique tub, black, with
clawed feet, like a fantastic,
fabulous Victorian monster,
some latter plumber included a
tracery of copper pipes up the
wall, for a shower,
and I emerge from its
tiny, hot spray, draw
the water-proof curtain and, to
astound me, some powerful
wizard's trick of transformation,
I thought you were
in the city, you
are there, waiting,
in the steam,
wearing only the chinese robe,
your long, black hair falling straight
to the shoulder,
you have a towel
in your hand, you
dry me, kneeling despite my
protestations, to bring its
rough, warm cloth across my
legs, I
embrace your head, suddenly, pull
you forward, so that you
rest your ear and your cheek and
your hair
against my stomach, still warm
from the water's edge

Caterpillar

I have always envied Alice who
on no logic but the promise of
a caterpillar did
take of it and eat (who
was it said, "life must be
chewed"?) I,
myself, am more
the rabbit type,
too wise to gamble, would
insist on FDA approval
of the mushroom,
and thus my life will
be spent in safety
and in holes

Chief

The chief of police I discover
while traveling in dreams.
He has concealed himself in a back room of the station,
or even a cell, and I find him
weeping immense tears
(the size of your fist, I swear, each of them)
over the death of a young officer
in the line of the duty,
while he sat in a car, and, at
22, at 3:00 AM, someone fired in
passing, though the window, while
he had been guarding the house of
a known offender, a
subsequent investigation by 60
minutes will allege the guilt
of the murdered man, for being
shot, without permission from eye-
witness news at 11

Education

each of us an undiscovered
country,
isolated, a
falling but not fallen angel
or
the hanged man of the tarot, suspended,
in his unshared and unknown universe,
each perception, interpretation,
unique,

so that, say, myth
itself is plastic, and you
select the wings, the flight, the sun,
I the maze, the wax, the minotaur,
and so each meeting
is an exploration, a journey.

I will teach you history, which
is to say,
fantasy (names of Gnostic
gods, the aspirations of the Byzantines)

You will teach me another
life
Swan boats,
the runner
on Alewife,
the

sound
of your
wings

bath 2

as a small, pale, pathetic substitute
for intimacy, i transform
you into that master-
piece of the advertisers art, the
bathing queen on
the front of the box of bath
beads, i
envision you as her, the model, your
hair in tight ringlets, in my imagination, your
eyes demure and cast
down, as though, so sensual was
your smallest act that earth,
air, water, fire brought
you close to orgasm, with
the white bubble bath foam up
as sweet, and flat, and rich as
a pornographer's image of the satin
sheet, i,
in my imagination, you bathe and
i sit cross-legged on the mat and i
read you my coy mistress the love
poetry of Tennyson and Dunne

Illicit Love

Revenge. Curious,
to realize that in her father's labors
was a form of infidelity
and vengeance, that
for every scene and confrontation, he
would deny her an hour, would
vanish in the direction of the office,
and, without the physics of sinning,
without that is, the finding of the mistress,
the contact, the heat of tissue against tissue,
illicit friction of mucus membranes,
expensive and embarrassing business of actual
adultery, behold! The Bride of
Frankenstein, a
paramour of paper and the spreadsheet software,
and thus, he revenged himself, on the face that
launched a thousand sulks.

ABOUT THE AUTHOR

Michael Jay Tucker is a writer, editor, and independent scholar. He lives in New Mexico with his wife, Martha, and Oreo, a Shitsu of extremely strong opinions. You may see more of his writing at his blog, explosive-cargo.blogspot.com, and at his Amazon author's page at http://www.amazon.com/-/e/B001KI3I6E